GOLD FEVER

Toby Sanders

Cover design by the author

ISBN: 9798863376547

Published by Amazon

FROM THE AUTHOR

Thanks for looking at my book! I'm a passionate self-published author on a mission to share my unique tales with readers like you. If you've enjoyed the journey so far, I'd be honoured if you could take a moment to leave a review on Amazon. To connect with my Amazon page, simply follow me on Twitter (X) for a quick and easy link @Toby_Author.

For Sedge, Theo & Elba

PROLOGUE

I couldn't turn, couldn't go back and couldn't see. Breathing was impossible and my lungs began to burn immediately. Had I taken a breath before I slid in? I couldn't remember and I floundered for a moment, knowing that this was death.

Was it so bad? At least I'd die whole, my body and mind connected. That was more than could be said for Gibbo, Martin, Jeff, Robbie, Andy and Mitchell. Not to mention the other SEALs and the unknown shooters who'd died in the small stretch of woodland that had clung to the side of the raging Nahanni. I wondered briefly who they were, it seemed important to remember everyone in my final thoughts. A half second later that seemed stupid. After all, this was my death and I didn't have to share it with anyone...

CHAPTER 1

The best thing about serving in the British Army Reserve is that when the inevitable happens and the army frustrates you to the point you're considering punching the next officer, Sergeant or sneering Corporal who even dares to make eye contact, is that there's nothing to stop you up and leaving whenever you want.

The only time a STAB (Stupid Territorial Army Bastard) as we're affectionately known to the regular army *can't* leave, is when we're mobilised. Then we're contracted to remain at our post lest we find ourselves detained at His Majesty's pleasure.

As it happened, my time in the Honourable Artillery Company coincided with what was bloody nearly World War Three. When I volunteered to be sent to the growing conflict in Europe, I spent more than a little time wondering just what the hell I was letting myself in for. Cutting around the grounds of the HAC where my para smock, maroon beret and blue wings earned me a certain amount of respect was one thing but, going away to war with *real* soldiers was a whole different ball game.

In the reserve, we're constantly berated, belittled (and sometimes encouraged) to meet the standard of our regular army counterparts. "You's are fookin' dog-shit!" our odious PSI (Permanent Staff Instructor), Sergeant Gibbo would bawl at us during our recruits' training. Gibbo was a thickset northerner hailing from the Coldstream Guards and he made it clear from the moment he laid eyes on our sorry looking platoon in our badly ironed kit, that we were dirt and he, in his own words, was the *ultimate* soldier.

Now, you might point out that the army is *supposed* to be hard and having a tough instructor is the most effective way of making good recruits. Maybe. The problem was, Gibbo had been sent here on a two year posting as a Sergeant. When he left, he'd go back to his battalion and he'd be promoted to Colour Sergeant. It was a good career move but he seemed to resent being around us from the start and made it his personal mission to take his frustrations out on us.

Looking back now with the benefit of six years of service, I can see some of his frustration. After all, the system of sending permanent staff to ensure the training of the reserve meets the regular army's standards is a logical one. But many PSIs find themselves struggling to fit in with the civvie/reservist culture and most simply don't comprehend that we don't *have* to turn up to our training. The usual army method of giving soldiers a time and a place to be and punishing them when they turn up late is a little difficult to apply when half the troops don't turn up at all.

But still, Gibbo went far beyond the usual frustrations of the permanent staff – most of whom I'll point out are excellent human beings, very engaged with the training they deliver and all round decent blokes – because he actually seemed to *hate* us.

"You's are fookin dog-shit!" he bawled at us as we stood stiffly to attention on first parade, midway through our recruits course "If any of you's ever turn up in my unit dressed like that, I'd fookin kill ya!"

He glared at us, daring us to meet his eye. Even though I was staring a foot over his head, I felt his gaze rest on me and he took a few quick steps over to where I stood in the middle rank of B Section.

"Stryker!" he hissed at me in his thick accent.

"Sergeant?"

"You don't fookin like me, do you?"

I opened my mouth, gaping stupidly like a fish as I sought to avoid the trap.

"Fookin posh southern poofter." He stalked away to berate another recruit. But there it was. He didn't like me because I sounded posh and I had grown up on the south coast where my parents had bought me the best education they could afford. I was in the HAC, the oldest and most prestigious regiment in the British Army and I was privileged. So, Gibbo hated me.

Throughout the six months of our recruits course, he pushed each one of us to the limit. On our penultimate training weekend which was an intense forty-eight hours of sleep deprivation and constant movement he seemed to shout at us without pause for every minute of every day. Midway through Saturday, four of our recruits snapped. One threw his rifle into a gorse bush and walked off. Later we heard he'd got a taxi back to London and the Royal Military Police were investigating him. Two others marched back to the car park where the coach had dropped us off Friday night and sat down on their bergans, refusing to move. The platoon commander didn't waste his scarce energy on them, instead leaving them to sulk in the driving rain. The fourth, a quiet Essex lad named Thompson, punched Gibbo in the jaw.

For reasons that I'm certain make sense to overpaid senior officers and civil servants, the army reserve never teaches its soldiers hand to hand combat. We spend a few hours learning how to operate our rifles, they teach us the theory of how to shoot and if you're lucky, you get to shoot at least two magazines per year. But otherwise, we have precious little training to defend ourselves. And so, when Thompson snapped and punched the Sergeant as Gibbo was screaming in his face, we all held our breaths, wondering if he'd finally stopped the bullying brute.

Instead, Gibbo shook the blow off as though it were a mere mosquito bite. Next second, he'd got Thompson in a choke hold, kicked his right leg out and had him on the floor. It was so quick and violent that the rush of rebellion that the rest of the platoon had shared was cooled in a moment. As Thompson turned purple, then white, we all stared in stupefied amazement until one of the other corporals arrived and shouted at Gibbo to stop. Thompson was kicked off the course after that and Gibbo wasn't charged as it was determined to be genuine self-defence.

So, that was my only exposure to the regular army until I put my name down to fight with them. In my worst nightmares as the date for my pre-deployment training approached, I was surrounded by a thousand Gibbo's, all of them hating me for daring to be a STAB in their midst. The vague protection of my Lance-Sergeant rank gave me little comfort. I told my boss, Major Mullen who'd served ten years in Sixteen Air Assault Brigade before moving to the HAC and he listened seriously before asking me if I'd gone to boarding school. More than a little confused I replied that I had and Major Mullen asked me if I'd enjoyed my time in education. "Yes, Sir." I replied and he gave me a warm smile and told me that the army was the same, the only difference being there were more northerners and shooting in the army.

Not particularly reassured I arrived at Finsbury Barracks one foggy Saturday to see the other four HAC volunteers standing with nervous excitement in front of their piles of kit.

"Reckon they'll do some kind of induction?" asked Smithy, a fresh faced Trooper who, like me, was in the Spec Inf Company.

"Inductions are illegal." Moore, a rotund Lance-Corporal from A Battery was shaking his head "They aren't allowed to do anything to us. And if they do? Just tell one of the officers."

Privately, I thought that was a pretty bloody stupid way to be approaching the whole thing but Moore was pale faced and I noticed his hands were shaking with nerves so I left him alone. As usual, the minibus that was supposed to drive us to the training area in the midlands was delayed. The bus had been booked by the MTWO (motor transport warrant officer) but there were no drivers. When the red faced NCO came stomping over to demand why we hadn't left yet, we explained the issue.

"Stryker." He jabbed a finger in my chest "You've done the course, ain't you?"

I replied that I had indeed got the necessary category D licence but it had been over three years since I'd driven a minibus and more than six months since I'd driven anything, given that I lived in London.

"Don't matter. You're driving now."

And that was it. Fortunately, I managed not to crash although there were a few hairy moments as we navigated Old Street roundabout with its eternal road works. I pulled out in front of a hefty looking lorry earning a blare of the horn from the driver. I shot him the finger in return and then broke the speed limit to get away from him. Perhaps not the most courageous or auspicious start to my war fighting career, but such is life within the M25.

The training camp when we finally arrived was neat, orderly and surprisingly quiet. The only real sound was the distinct crack of rifles firing although from the low rate of fire they were clearly on a range rather than a tactical manoeuvre.

"Who are you?" a thin man with the three pips of a Captain had appeared out of nowhere as I exited the minibus, stiff from the long motorway drive. I hastened to stand to attention.

"Lance-Sergeant Stryker, Sir. Honourable Artillery Company."

"Ah. The Spec Inf chaps? You're over there." He gestured at a building that looked like a 1960's council block "Look for Sergeant Coln. Make sure you and your blokes all get a bunk, a locker and you know where the scoff house, armoury and ablutions are. Got it?"

"Sir." I replied in the affirmative although my mind was racing and I could hardly remember which building he'd pointed at, let alone the name of the man I was supposed to report to. Still, the Captain was marching away, apparently under the impression I'd understood and I turned hopefully to the rest of the HAC blokes to see Moore was already heading towards one of the buildings. Grateful that someone had been listening, I locked the minibus and followed him, overtaking him halfway to make sure I was the first into the accomodation.

The door was locked. That was a good start but after a knock, it was opened by a shirtless and skinny looking Private who gaped at us as I explained who we were. He jerked a thumb over his shoulder and then scurried away into a room, the door of which was wedged open with someone's bergan. Laden with our kit, we shuffled our way awkwardly down a linoleum floored corridor and glanced into the open room as we passed. It was filled with about twenty metal cots and a similar number of soldiers inside, all of whom were gathered together in a knot, staring silently at us as we passed.

"Morning." I called, nodding to them. There was no response but I persevered "Anyone know where Sergeant Coln is?"

"Not in here, Sir. This is blokes' accommodation." someone replied and I winced as I realised with my accent and civvy clothes they'd mistaken me for an officer.

"I'm a Lance-Sergeant by the way." I pointed out, more than a little awkwardly but again there was no response "Where can we find him?"

"Who?"

"Sergeant Coln." I resisted the urge to close my eyes at the density of the question.

"S'arnt Coln's not in here."

"Yes, I know that. Where is he?" I was still speaking to the entire room rather than one individual and I couldn't even have said which of the soldiers was responding to me.

"She's in the female accommodation."

That explained the confusion. Coln was a female and so would not be anywhere near this block. Rolling my eyes in frustration, I tried a different tack "Are there any empty bunks in here?"

"Not in here, Sergeant." This time I saw the lad who spoke and he pointed at the plainly full room.

"I meant in this building."

"Oh. Yeah, go down the corridor."

"Thanks." We continued our shuffling walk, laden with bergans and civvie kit until we found a room identical to the first except it was empty. A thin layer of dust covered the rubber mattresses in here and I immediately sneezed as I dumped my bergan onto the bed.

"What's our next timing?" Smithy asked, looking around expectantly.

"What part of that conversation made you think I know anything about anything?" I replied testily and he lowered his gaze, sitting down on his bed and leaning back against his bed.

Oh, to be a Trooper again, bereft of responsibilities!

I pulled on my uniform, checking my boots were polished and the creases on my trousers were sharp and, dragging an unwilling Smithy along, marched out to find the elusive Sergeant Coln.

Instead, I got a man about half my height and at least twice my width with the crown of a WO2 shouting at me from across the tarmac where we'd parked the minibus.

"Is this your shagging wagon?"

"Er – yes, Sir."

"Move it!"

I hastened over to the vehicle "Where to, Sir?"

"There's no shagging parking here!"

"Yes - where should I move it to?"

He looked flummoxed, blinking at me several times. Clearly, moving the vehicle had been the object of his ire and a solution to where to take it had not occurred.

"Where's it come from?"

"We brought it up from London. Our driver didn't turn up so I drove."

"Who are you?"

"Lance-sergeant Stryker, HAC. We've just arrived for pre-deployment training."

"Oh…"

"Is there a car park, Sir?"

"Yes."

I held my patience and looked around as though a sign would be visible "I don't suppose you know where it is, do you, Sir?" I pressed in my most agreeable tone of voice. To my surprise, he did and heaved his bulk into the passenger seat with a groan of effort. For the next seven or eight minutes I drove us around the camp following his directions as he showed us the armoury, the ranges, the scoff house, the ablutions, the guard room and every other building on the camp. The shouty, sweary attitude vanished completely to be replaced by an affable, friendly demeanour that had me completely baffled. There was in fact a car park and there was plenty of space. I had to display my name and rank in the windscreen and the WO2 even provided me with paper and a marker pen to complete this, all the while chatting to me merrily about the goings on of the camp.

He was interrupted by a female voice calling over to Smithy who I'd forgotten was with us and the WO2 shut up mid-sentence, turning to introduce Sergeant Coln who nodded a greeting to me before steering us away from the warrant officer.

"Yeah, he's a right talker." she indicated the loquacious WO2 "You two are with us, right?" she indicated the Spec Inf insignia on our arms and we nodded our agreement "Alright. Which block are you in?" when we told her she shook her head and so half an hour later, sweating badly now under the strain of our kit we moved into another building where we were treated to our own individual rooms with en-suite bathrooms.

Gucci!

As I went to sleep that night, not bothering with the ear plugs I'd assumed would be a must-have, I reflected that perhaps Gibbo was a bad example of the regular army and that maybe the next few months wouldn't be too bad. It was a badly needed optimism that lowered my stress levels a few degrees although Smithy banging on my door at a quarter past midnight sent them rocketing back up.

"Beer?" he held out a can he'd clearly stashed inside his kit.

"It's bloody quarter past midnight, Smithy."

He looked perplexed "I know."

I sighed "Look, mate. I know we want to have fun on this gig but let's not turn up pissed on our first morning, eh?"

He looked at the can in his hand "I've only got the two of them."

The young lad looked so disconsolate that I immediately felt like a total idiot and I opened the door fully, rolling my eyes.

Turned out that one of Coln's blokes was passing and he saw the beers, vanishing to return a moment later with six other soldiers, each sporting a crate of lager which cheered Smithy up immensely. Trying to nurse my drink and not annihilate my head for the next morning, I soon found myself challenged to an arm wrestle which I lost, a press up competition which I won and then a contest to see who could drink four cans of cheap lager the fastest which frankly, nobody won.

My headache began to set in about 0300 the next morning and by 0500 when my small room was finally empty save for the stink of beer and regret, it was pounding like a drum. Still, there were worse ways to start a new job.

CHAPTER 2

Two hours later when Smithy gallantly dragged me into the scoff house for a sorry breakfast of hash browns, bacon and beans, my regrets were so strong I had half a mind to mount the minibus and drive myself home. Instead, a chipper looking Coln informed us to pack our wet and warm kit for a long day on the range.

As we worked our way through a long and drizzly day outdoors, the similarities between public school and the army became apparent. The officers and Senior NCO's hung around the edges of the range, talking in small groups much like the teachers on a sports field. To my surprise, they were welcoming, asking probing questions about the HAC and the reserve. It was a tough concept for them to grasp, the idea that I, a civilian, could do the same job as them only two hours training per week and one short weekend per month. Still, when I got behind the stock of the SA80 they saw I could shoot and I think they were quietly impressed and I explained my passion for shooting, having represented my local club back in London at several national and international events.

This resulted in some competition. As the blokes crammed under the rusty troop shelter and forced down the mysterious brown substance known in the army as 'range stew', I and a stocky brute of a Sergeant named Fletcher went out to the range to run through a complex set of shoots which the Range Officer seemed to be making up on the spot. Still, I aced every part, knocking the targets down even at the longest range without much difficulty, glad that I had a skill I could rely on.

"You're good, Stryker." Fletcher held out a grudging hand as he admitted defeat. To my surprise, the rest of Coln's troops from the Spec Inf Coy gave a round of applause and I blushed, suddenly hoping I hadn't been showing off.

I made some humble comments which provoked laughter from Fletcher who despite his appearance had a far worse bark than bite as he and I hunkered over our questionable lunch in the troop shelter.

"Do you know Gibbo?" Fletcher asked casually. My heart rate actually spiked at his words and I did not look away from the 'watch and shoot' detail being run a few metres ahead of me.

"You a friend of his?" I replied, cautiously.

"Not really." Fletcher seemed to just be making conversation "Me 'n him was recruits together. I know he went to you's down at the HAC for a couple of years. Wondered if you'd met him."

I explained he was the PSI on my recruit's course which earned me a wince of sympathy from Fletcher.

"He don't like STAB's." Fletcher shook his head.

"No. He wasn't my favourite." I was cautious not to slag Gibbo off. For all I knew, Fletcher was his BFF but he shocked me by spinning off on a rant about Gibbo, telling me how the man had been demoted for bullying on two occasions and had been passed around from pillar to post in an attempt to keep him out of trouble.

"Where is he now?" my question had a certain weight to it, I half expected Fletcher to announce that Gibbo was attached to our mobilisation, something that probably would have led me to hand over my MOD 90 ID card and risk the wrath of Colchester military prison.

"22." Was the laconic reply.

"SAS?" I asked.

"Who else? He passed Selection a couple of years back."

For some reason, that sent warm fuzzy feelings through me. The chances now of me ever running into Gibbo were slim to none because at that time as we ramped up to fight in Europe, 22 SAS were prosecuting a semi-legal guerrilla campaign against the enemy and from the rumours that made it to my ears, they were in it for the duration.

I made some comment about the Special Forces to Fletcher and he nodded seriously "I reckon he's a good fit. Wouldn't want to cross him. Tough bastard, that Gibbo. SF needs blokes like that now. You ever thought of joining?"

"The SAS? Never." I shook my head. The SF were open to reservists but the time commitment required to get a part-time soldier to the level of the finest fighting force in the world was ludicrous and although I'd never had a serious civilian career to speak of, I resented the thought that the army could have such a hold over my spare time.

"Thought about giving it a go next year myself." Fletcher mused and I restrained myself from raising an eyebrow, his stocky physique not belying much confidence in his physical ability. Still, I stayed tactful with the man, appreciating his friendly demeanour.

Coln had us move onto a tactical shoot, running through a complex series of live fire scenarios in urban settings which was likely to be the bulk of the combat we saw in Europe. The enemy's strategy had so far been simple, although effective and seizing key buildings in towns and cities had given them an efficient control over vast swathes of previously free countryside which was why our leaders in Britain had put such a heavy emphasis on building up our Spec Inf capability. It probably helped that they threw money at our kit and equipment demands meaning that even the unqualified candidates on our gruelling training cadre were dressed like US Navy Seals. Feeling like you looked the part was certainly a big step in the direction of true professionalism.

I ran through a few of the scenarios at the head of a small team, cursing my throbbing head and Smithy's enthusiasm. Afterwards, we took turns to observe each other operate and I was pleased to see the HAC blokes held their own against the regular soldiers, even outpacing them a few times although Moore sweated and panted his way through the buildings.

"Where'd you say you go shooting again?" asked Fletcher as I corrected one of the junior soldiers on his marksmanship principles and I explained how a few of us from the HAC travelled regularly to eastern Europe or the US to participate in practical and tactical shooting events.

"Hoping it might pay off now." I told Fletcher, referring to our upcoming deployment.

He looked serious "Word around camp is they're planning a big push. There's a big drive in recruitment for Spec Inf now, we've got four cadres coming through in the next three months alone."

"Three months?" I asked in surprise "The war might be over in three months!"

Fletcher gave me a significant look "Yeah, or they might suddenly need to fill a lot of vacant jobs."

I gulped as I realised what he meant and the full realisation that I was going to war hit me. I tried to shake the feeling as Fletcher gave me a knowing grimace.

My nervousness grew as the date for our mobilisation approached. Unheeding, the small platoon found its feet and under the leadership of Sergeant Coln, who insisted we all call her by her first name, Annie, we fostered a relationship of professionalism and harmony, learning to operate together smoothly. But I was clearly not alone in my anxiety and the closer we got to shipping out, the more unruly the blokes became. Fletcher and Moore got into a screaming row over a place in the scoff-house queue and had to be pulled apart. One of the Privates, a spotty nineteen year old named Foster had a negligent discharge on the range which nearly killed Annie and resulted in him being booted out of the platoon. That was the same day that Smithy approached me and said he wanted to go home.

"Why?" I asked, genuinely puzzled. Smithy was young, fit and seemingly carefree. He'd blitzed through every part of our training with ease, his endless banter keeping our morale up.

"I just – I keep thinking about home and how my parents

would feel if I were killed." he muttered, staring at the floor in my room where he blocked the doorway.

"You aren't going –" I began but he shook his head.

"It's possible. Blokes are getting killed every day out there. If this war really kicks off..." he trailed off.

"Smithy, remember what you're here for." I stood, facing him down "If this war really kicks off then you're going to be in it, whether you like it or not. Another European conflict will going to sweep across the whole continent and it'll reach your home whether you like it or not."

He looked up at me, dully.

"Your Mum and Dad will need you to defend them, so at the very least you can come and get some experience before you have to do that. Got it?"

He nodded at me and that was it. I never heard him complain again but I kept a close eye on him, making certain I kept the younger man busy and praised him for his good work. It wasn't easy though, the change of pace from civilian life to the non-stop training. I was glad to be out of my boring office job where mindless hours spent staring at data charts was what had driven me into the reserves in the first place but I found myself missing the easy parts, three hour lunch breaks in the pub, 'popping out' for a coffee and spending the morning wandering around London. Those things just didn't happen in the army and the regulars laughed when I told them although in their defence, the working day when we were in camp was 0900 to 1600 at the longest and Fridays, we finished just after lunch. That was a welcome culture shock but we soon settled into it.

At T-minus three weeks to our deployment date, we had a 'smoker' which Moore organised, piling tureens of sausages, jerk chicken and charred burgers which were devoured ravenously. The WO2 who'd yelled at me the first day appeared out of nowhere and scooped up enough food to feed a small elephant before sitting down to chatter amiably with the Spec Inf blokes. Recognising me, he beckoned me over to perch on the lowered tailgate of a Land Rover. Smithy came too, licking his fingers noisily as the warrant officer whose name I never got, spoiled everything.

"You're Stryker, aren't you?"

I confirmed that I was.

"You know you're being posted to another unit?"

I was flabbergasted and assumed there was some mistake. I told him I was a section commander in the Spec Inf platoon but he shook his head.

"That's why they want you to go. You know how the army works – it's all about your skill set! You've got data skills, don't you?"

Smithy had vanished to fetch Annie who stomped over immediately as I admitted data analysis was my day job.

"Right – charts and that. Pulling info apart and telling us what it means." It was plain the WO2 had no idea what the job actually was "It's gonna be a big part of this conflict, all the info that's being gathered before we go in shows us what and where the enemy is."

Annie frowned "That's intelligence, surely? Don't we have an Int Corps for that?"

The WO2 burped enormously before sucking on a chicken leg "Don't ask me. You know how it goes." he shot me a sly look "Probably your fault for being overqualified."

"This is rubbish!" I swore in frustration "What's the point in me being here all this time if I'm just going to be binned off?"

The WO2 shrugged "People cleverer than you and me make those decisions."

"Which unit is he going to?" Annie asked but the WO2 didn't know. He held up greasy hands in his defence.

"Don't shoot the messenger, Annie! Stryker here worked in data analysis in his civvie job. Someone, somewhere says they need a data analyst who's Para trained!"

"We can't just lose Liam now! We could be at war in three weeks!"

The WO2 stuffed a piece of chicken into his mouth as though it might take flight "I know!" he swallowed hugely "Bloody stupid, isn't it?"

But there was nothing for it. The next day the same Captain who'd greeted us on arrival summoned me to his office to give me the formal briefing, calling my boss Major Mullen back at the HAC to advise him of the change. I complained bitterly to both men, explaining my position and how tightly the platoon was bound to one another. Mullen promised to make a few calls but I didn't cross my fingers.

The platoon sulked that day, doing precious little work as I waited to hear back from Mullen. When he finally rang back, I stepped away from the other soldiers, moving around the corner of the building but I heard scuffling behind me and glanced back to see the blokes casually lounging just within earshot.

"I can't tell you a lot about who you're deploying with, " the Major began "it's a top-shelf opportunity though and you'll get a lot out of it."

I protested that I couldn't just abandon my troops this far into our training but Mullen cut me off.

"It's tough shit, Stryker. I'm sorry but the army has spoken. You're deploying tomorrow and –"

"Tomorrow?" a note of panic rose in my voice and Mullen paused for a moment before responding.

"Yes. Tomorrow. You've still got a wagon with you, correct? Good. You're to drive back down to the HAC and you'll be transported from here."

I didn't waste any more breath protesting but instead listened as I was given my orders. I trudged back to the platoon lines to deliver the bad news and the blokes stared at me glumly. There was a general air of mutiny until Annie appeared laden down with a crate of beers which cheered us all up immensely. To no-one's surprise, the WO2 appeared only seconds later to join in the block party and so it transpired that I spent the night before I went to war, absolutely hammered.

CHAPTER 3

I (gulp) drove myself and the minibus back down to London the following morning, stopping only for fuel and to vomit copiously in a crisp packet I'd balanced on my lap. I hit a not inconsiderable amount of traffic on the M25 which I'd expected although as we crawled along towards the junction, our progress got slower and slower. Finally, as the outside lane began to speed up and I signalled to pull out into the flow, we passed a bunch of army SV trucks, all of them with the canvas covers slung open at the rear. I peered into the gloomy interior as I passed and spotted men, women and children, all with bundles over their laps and expressions of dejected defeat on their faces.

Refugees.

They were the first I'd seen and from the volume of people in the convoy, it didn't look like they were the last. The war in Europe had seemed a distant thing, well out of reach, even as we worked through our preparations to deploy but now, seeing the tears on the face of an old woman, her hair grey and matted, it became very real. I felt a shiver run down my spine at the thought of what lay before me.

I tried not to think of Smithy and his fears. The young lad had perked up in the past couple of days, looking more like his old self as he'd jumped into training with a will but, as I'd left he'd looked utterly dejected. I'd asked Annie to keep an eye on him but I couldn't shake the feeling that I was abandoning my troops.

Fortunately, at that moment an Audi R8 painted in a tacky turquoise swung in front of me with a blare of London angst and I consoled myself by cursing the driver, his poor motoring skills and his general ancestry until my blood pressure dropped. He carried on regardless, swooping through the traffic without a care for those of us suffering in the gridlock.

As I pulled through the security checkpoint onto the parade square of Finsbury Barracks, I saw the Sergeant Major, a Welsh Guardsman named (of all things) Davies who eyeballed me the moment I appeared and flagged me down.

"Who are you?" he barked by way of greeting. Charming chap.

"Lance-Sergeant Stryker, Sir." I tried not to breathe in his direction, well aware of the booze weighing down my personality that morning.

"You're late!"

I looked at my watch "I was told 1000, Sir."

That resulted in some mostly unintelligible Welsh grumblings interspersed with a handful of very English curses which were no doubt well meant but I let them pass over me.

"Right, park the wagon, get your kit and onto the field." He gestured at the artillery gardens, our regiment's training area-come-sports pitch which was empty aside from the usual pair of rugby goals.

"Sir?" I asked but the Sergeant Major had turned, shouting at a pair of unfortunate Troopers who'd dawdled in front of the barracks for too long. Wondering why he'd wasted my precious youth with his nonsense, I parked, deposited the key in the guard room and then made my down onto the gardens where I sank down onto my bergan, my head throbbing with alcohol withdrawal.

"Stryker? Lance-Sergeant Stryker?" a voice called and I jumped, sitting bolt upright and peering around to see a short man who, aside from the Crye Precision clothing he was wearing looked about as far from a soldier as it was possible to be. Squat, with an odd shape to his torso that at first appeared to be a well-earned beer gut but on closer inspection turned out to be a frame so packed with muscle it was hard to tell there were organs pumping beneath it. He had a smattering of stubble on his cheeks and chin, hardly long enough to count as a beard.

He had almost no neck, and his forehead was concentrated into a permanent frown. It was only his eyes that belied the man behind the carefully cultivated exterior. They were hard as iron, a pale blue that gripped my own gaze immediately and commanded total attention. His uniform and bearing told me that this man was Special Forces and I blinked, holding out my hand and trying not to breathe my hangover into his face.

"I'm Solly. 22 SAS." he shook with a friendly grin.

"Liam Stryker. HAC."

"You're Spec Inf? Nice. I was before I went SF. Good job to have. Sorry you got pulled off your mobilisation."

"No dramas." my confusion must have shown on my face because he gave a small chuckle, dumping his considerably lighter kit bags down beside mine.

"Yeah, bit of a cluster, I'm afraid. You might not get time for a full briefing so I'll give you the long and short."

He did. As it turned out, Solly (not his real name) had been in the Regiment eight years and was now in charge of this particular operation. He was responsible for me being pulled away from my platoon, a fact that he went out of his way to apologise for, commiserating at the ability of the army to mess its soldiers around.

"Still," he continued as we stood, somewhat lamely in the empty gardens "you'll come back from this the best soldier in the HAC. Next couple of weeks we're really going to push you to match the standard we need. You've got your wings – " he indicated the blue para wings on my shoulder "but when's the last time you jumped?"

When I confessed I hadn't done a parachute jump since passing the jumps course two years ago at Brize Norton he gave a derisive snort, promising that I'd spend more of the next two weeks falling to earth than I would actually standing on it.

"It's a precise drop we're doing and I can't risk you any errors."

"What do you need me for?" I asked him, my patience and hangover getting the better of me.

Somewhat frustratingly, I think that if I write the full details down here, the Ministry of Defence in their infinite wisdom will redact the entire book. As circumstances stand, the chances of this tome ever seeing the light of day again are slim, but in the interests of giving it my best shot, I'll play the game a little here and suffice it to say that the SAS needed me to deploy to the European theatre to work with data they were gathering. It's a little cryptic, but the value of this data was the difference between two world wars, or three. That is to say, if our mission failed, the world might end in a nuclear fireball the likes of which those mugs in the cold war could never have imagined.

So, no pressure.

"Here we are." Solly pointed at the sky with a stubby, gnarled finger and a moment later, what I'd thought was the pounding in my head turned out to be the double rotors of a Chinook helicopter which swooped around the towering brutalist icons of the Barbican and then, after much hovering and dust blowing, landed in front of us on the gardens.

Solly led me forward as I scooped up my kit and hurried towards the great snarling beast. The heat of the exhaust struck me and I felt another wave of nausea, pausing to vomit by the lowered ramp. I made my way up into the interior, eyes streaming, to see the faces of the toughest, meanest bunch of 'operators' you've ever seen.

Every one of them killing themselves laughing at me.

I dropped my gaze, face burning and fell into a seat, dropping my kit on the metal floor before me. I busied myself searching for my ear defence as I felt the glances and shouted jibes build in the cabin of the chinook which lifted off and swung around, the back door still open. So engrossed in my task was I that I totally missed the spectacular panorama of the city passing below me and by the time I looked out of the helo, the city had given way to rolling fields and the smiles of the SAS team had finally faded.

So, to summarise, I was pulled out of my platoon, told I was deploying with the SAS, flown by chinook out of London and next thing I knew, I was being dropped into a war zone by parachute. All in a day's work, I suppose and it truly makes for a fascinating read but the title of this book is 'Headless Gold' and you didn't come here to hear about my 'war' which lasted eight months, squished into the damp concrete of an abandoned Soviet bunker in Europe, 'analysing data' for the British Special Forces. Whilst it would make for an excellent tale, as previously mentioned I think the MOD would redact the entire book and were I ever to publish it, I'd end up in prison for the rest of my life and frankly, the story of the Headless Valley is what I'm here to tell. So, lets skip forward eight months in our narrative from the chinook flight out of the HAC to an 'undisclosed location' in Europe where we had just prevented the outbreak of a third world war.

CHAPTER 4

The bunker we called 'home' was a former KGB outpost. It had housed a couple of hundred operatives behind the iron curtain who'd tapped into the communications of the entire continent. Once the USSR collapsed, it, like many other facilities like it was emptied of any useful equipment and data and sealed. British intelligence became aware of it sometime before our deployment and a single operative from MI6 was sent to use local support to make it operational again. So, for the eight months we lived in the dark and gloomy communist stronghold, we rubbed shoulders in the corridors with locals who brought us food, moonshine and most importantly, kept the enemy from learning our location. Solly and his blokes made the place safer than Fort Knox. I can remember wondering about six weeks in whether or not it was really secure and learned the hard way when I woke in the night, busting for a piss and lit a bine (smoke) only to be bundled and almost shot by one of his blokes who came out of the darkness like a fairy tale monster.

After that, I had a lot more respect for Solly and in the time I wasn't doing my day job, I asked the guys to teach me how to be a better soldier. I fancy that I scratched the surface of how these master warriors earned their reputation but I confess to being a long way from their standard. Still, I consoled myself smoking the black market bines the locals sold us, doing my best to pick up the language and blushing at the laughter of the local women as I failed to flirt with the few who dared approach. Sadly, most looked like carthorses with personalities to match but after a few months I became rather enamoured of them although I never managed anything more than a deep smile.

Shame.

Two nights before we were due to leave the bunker, I came across a pair of the locals who'd just been escorted in by Solly. They greeted me warmly in the odd mixture of English and the local dialect which between the four of us, we used to communicate. The custom here was for every conversation to begin and end with a drink, and manners apparently dictated that the invitee should provide the booze to their host. Seeing as we only ever invited the locals here, that left us on the receiving end every time. I'd argue this is the greatest social custom our species has ever come up with.

As the locals poured the suspiciously innocent looking liquid into four battered tin cups, Solly and I took our shots. He didn't flinch as the raw spirit went down but I had to fight not to fall over or be sick or have a heart attack. The stuff could easily have been sold from a petrol station pump anywhere in the UK and you'd have been none the wiser. Still, the locals were being friendly and we waited through the usual pleasantries to discover that the pair had come to say goodbye, knowing that we were leaving because NATO tanks had finally reached their village.

"We want to thank you." was the general theme of the conversation and so Solly, being a top bloke called for most of his guys to come in, leaving only a few to keep watch.

After the slow translations of thanks, we settled down to a good long chat and I found myself speaking to the older of the two locals, a whitebeard who we'll just call Vlad. Vlad was a rotund man with leathery skin and an endless supply of stories. I'd loved listening to him spin a yarn as my command of the language and his of mine grew stronger but now, as the dark grew outside the bunker, he was the one who told us the story of the Headless Valley.

Let's interject here and explain that I am, by any description, a sceptic. I don't believe in ghosts, ghouls, goblins, hobgoblins, poltergeists, demons, spirits, UFO's, aliens, monsters or any other fantasy beasty. I hate horror movies, I despise conspiracy theories and I point and laugh at credulous fools who believe them.

It was some surprise then to find myself enraptured by Vlad's tale. Maybe he was just a good storyteller but seriously, it was compelling as anything. See for yourself:

Back in the 1800's three brothers living in Canada decided to head into a valley which was formed by the Nahanni river. Now, bits of the valley had been explored already but as far as the three brothers knew, no-one had yet found gold there. This being the middle of the Gold Rush in the USA and sensing an opportunity to strike it rich, the brothers began planning an expedition into the valley. They knew the river snaked its way through the mountains up to the Virgina Falls and reasoned that the flow of that cascade would stir up gold dust if there were any to be found. After speaking to a few local prospectors, the brothers learned that gold dust, when it's stirred up by white water is then transported downstream where it is deposited as sediment.

To the brothers, this was excellent news. It meant they'd have less distance to travel before they found a site to pan for gold. And so, they purchased a good boat and began to travel upstream, heading into the valley. On the way, they passed a few landmarks. The entrance to the Headless Valley is marked by the Kraus hot springs and the brothers left the stink of sulphur behind them as they moved up the river. Next, they rowed into a canyon with towering rock faces on either side casting them into a perpetual gloom even during the day. There was no shoreline here, no place for them to beach their boat and so the brothers continued paddling, moving through the shadows.

They came to a second canyon and here the water was as deep as the towering cliffs above them. Great cave networks filled the sheer rock faces, their depths unexplored by man. Sunlight did not reach the water's surface and the three brothers shivered as they searched for a spot to land their boat and strike their fortune. Finally, a strip of woodland appeared around a bend in the river and the brothers paddled furiously to reach it, grounding their boat on the rough shoreline. Safely out of the water, they pulled their sluices from the boat and waded out into the shallows. Not a moment later, sluices filled with gold dust. Jubilant, they made camp and slept through that night, their minds filled with images of shining riches.

When they left the valley, laden down with their gold they struck a rock and their boat sank, destroying many of their supplies and spilling all of their gold into the Nahanni river. Furious, the three men returned to their camp and set their sluices but now there was no gold to be had. Low on supplies and with winter approaching, they fashioned a new boat from timber they'd cut from the trees on the bank and returned home, empty handed.

Next season, two of the brothers decided to return to the valley in search of more Gold leaving their elder brother behind. They planned to be gone for at least one year, maybe more and they left in good spirits. A year passed, then two and by the third summer, the elder brother who had remained behind purchased a boat and with other men from the town set out to find his two younger siblings. In the second canyon, they came upon the two younger brothers – or rather, they came upon what was left of them. Two headless corpses lay in the remnants of their camp, the necks sliced cleanly and the bodies otherwise unmarked. Carved into the wood of a nearby tree was the ominous message 'We have found a fine prospect'.

Now, as I said, I'm a sceptic of the first order. I don't believe in head-eating monsters but the old geezer had the gift of the gab, despite the language barrier and maybe it was just the combination of being so far from home, the stress of the past few months and the company I was in but I found myself holding my breath, waiting for Vlad to tell us more. A shiver ran down my spine.

Later, years later, another prospector sought to try his luck in the Nahanni valley. He settled in second canyon, naming it Gold Creek and built himself a sturdy cabin to survive the winter. Well provisioned with supplies and armed with a rifle, he set his sluices and panned for gold. When he failed to return after the predicted two seasons, a rescue party from the Royal Canadian Mountain Police set out to search for the man and quickly came across the cabin he'd built, finding it burned to the ground. Presuming some terrible accident had occurred they stirred the ashes, searching for the missing prospector. His charred skeleton lay beneath the collapsed beams, almost perfectly intact with the scorched remnants of his clothes around him. His head, however, was missing. The vertebrae of the neck had been sliced cleanly and despite bringing dogs and combing the area, the Mounties found no trace of his head.

In the middle of the twentieth century, as the world eased from the destruction of the second world war, a fourth prospector set out to try his luck. He was found by trappers, laid out neatly in his camp with his head cleanly separated from the body. The trappers searched but never found the head.

Authorities investigated, writers and journalists hounded the locals for rumours and hearsay. What they found was not just the stories of four headless men found in second canyon, but half a hundred men who had vanished in the canyon carved by the Nahanni river. Indeed, the river itself is named for a local tribe who were reputed to be a fierce, violent race, feared by natives and settlers alike. That is, until the latter part of the frontier period when they too succumbed to the dangers of the valley and vanished without a trace.

No tribe moved in to claim the empty land but oral traditions told it to be a land of ghosts and demons. They told that the river was old, older than the canyon itself, having flowed through the land before the mountains were even pushed up and carving the modern canyon as the rocky hills were formed.

Another shiver down my spine. In my mind, towering cave-filled bluffs blotted out the sun as foolhardy frontiersmen paddled along ice cold water, their eyes twitching for danger in the darkness. But among the dark was the glint of a golden metal, flakes floating on the surface of the water whilst monsters rustled the towering trees on the bank.

Urgh.

Vlad, having scared the bejesus out of me, chose that moment to leave abruptly, taking his younger friend with him. With many bows and smiles and handshakes, they left the bunker and we settled down for the next morning when we were due to hand over to a second team. I was bound for home and I'd be mighty glad to see the lights of London but the allure of the city faded as I sat in the gloom of my makeshift bedroom. A pair of the SAS blokes were still sitting around, laughing about the story Vlad had told. One of them, a towering Scot who we'll call 'Doug' called over to me.

"Oi, STAB! You gonna go gold hunting when you get back?"

"Might do. You lot going to come and watch my back?"

He guffawed at that "Aye! Might be you'll cut me a slice of what you find and I'll not slot you and leave you for the river. Mebbe I'll even leave your head!" he snorted and turned away.

"Why not though?" I asked "We take an SAS team there, I reckon we could live out for a few months. With modern technology I bet we'd find more gold than anyone else has. We could even get a helicopter in rather than messing around with the river."

"Aye..." Doug looked pensive for a moment but then Solly called his name and he turned to leave "Ask the boss about it, STAB. He's the man."

I asked Solly and he laughed "It's all very well being snuggled up in here with us but Canada has some wild bits. It's not a case of turn up and pitch a tent. That takes some serious preparation and it costs a lot to do that. Who's going to pay for you to go hunting some old legend?" he chuckled "Look, you're going home tomorrow. Focus on doing your job for the last day, yeah?"

"Alright."

London was waiting for me and so were my parents. It was bloody good to be home, I have to say but still, my dreams were filled with images of yellow metal.

CHAPTER 5

If you can cast your mind back to the first part of this story, you'll remember that I explained the benefit of being a reservist is that when the army inevitably decides to mess you around, you can just up and leave at any point. This was the exact scenario I found looming before me upon my return to the HAC. Firstly, Moore, the A Battery Lance-Corporal was now an A Battery Lance-Sergeant and didn't he know it. As I stepped out of the transport (sadly downgraded to a Land Rover this time), he approached and began demanding I clear the parade square as he was apparently thrashing some new recruits around. Blinking, I obliged, carrying my kit out of the way when he decided to bawl at me to hurry up.

"Exactly who are you speaking to?" I demanded, snapping.

"Just move!" he shouted back, the thirty or so recruits gawping as the two of us squared off.

"It's polite to say 'please'." I pointed out with no small measure of sarcasm "And you can piss off, you tubby idiot." That isn't quite what I said but it was words to that effect.

"Listen here –" he began, actually prodding a pudgy finger at my chest. Unfortunately, Moore and his newfound authority had overstepped the mark. I gripped his hand and stepped forward, twisting his wrist over in a tight lock one of Solly's guys had taught me and he gasped, his torso leaning over to follow. I stepped again and swept his foot from under him sending him crashing to the ground with a thump of spare flesh. Moore rolled like a beached walrus as a handful of the recruits came to pull us apart.

I stepped back and decided to make myself scarce. Moore was

red faced and looking mutinous but I ignored him, scooping up my kit and heading back up to the Spec Inf Coy locker room. There I got my second 'welcome home' because someone had emptied my locker and the kit I'd left secured there, was gone. In vain I strode around looking for the missing items but they were nowhere to be found and as it wasn't our usual training night, there was no-one else there to ask.

The door crashed open as I was considering throwing a few of the heavier items through the window for good measure and a female officer, bearing the three pips of a captain burst in. Hastily, I saluted as she regarded me coolly, informing me the new Sergeant-Major wanted to see me.

Memories of the previous Welsh Guardsman filled my mind as made my way down to his office only to discover that the new chap's predecessor had actually been the better of the two. He proceeded to lecture me for the next forty minutes on the differences between operational deployments and barracks life before telling me that I was still under mobilisation rules for the next four days and I was to spend those practicing drill for the medals parade the Commanding Officer was going to hold. Apparently, this was as a favour to me although as I'd been expecting to spend the next four days drunk out of my skull, it was hard to appreciate.

"Do you know how to receive an award?" the Sergeant Major demanded and I – stupid fool that I am – hesitated. That did it. He marched me outside and onto the parade square and had me for the next hour march up, crash to attention, and shake his hand before asking permission to carry on. A drill movement that took all of twenty steps and about thirty seconds to complete.

As I managed to negotiate a smoke break, I saw a ruddy faced Lance-Sergeant Moore emerge from the barracks and approach the Sergeant Major. Cursing inwardly, I continued smoking, affecting an air of nonchalance.

"Stryker!" the guardsman's voice cut across the parade square.

I stared truculently in response.

"On me, now!"

I moved slowly over, taking my time.

"Did you strike this man?"

"No, Sir." I replied truthfully.

"He says you did."

"Actually, I put him on the floor." I kept my tone mild.

"Why?"

I tried to pause to consider the most politic answer but Moore's stupid face annoyed me and my mouth didn't get the message "Because he's a fat, gobby tosspot, Sir and I'm embarrassed to wear the same uniform as him."

The Sergeant Major looked like he was going to have a stroke but instead began a rant, none of which I bothered to listen to. Instead, I stared at the gates of the HAC, wondering what in the Hell I was doing standing listening to this clown when the joys of civilian life awaited. The more I thought about it, the more compelling the idea became and it was somewhere around here that I realised there wasn't anything else for me here.

"Yeah, whatever, Sir." I cut across the Sergeant Major mid rant "The idiot deserved it and frankly, I've had enough." I reached into my pocket, pulled out my wallet and produced my MOD 90 ID card "Here you go. Cheerio." I tossed the ID card to the gaping Sergeant Major and shoulder barged Moore out of the way. I ignored the rising fury of the tubby Lance-Sergeant behind me and for some reason, the Sergeant Major remained silent. Perhaps he'd seen too many blokes snap in the past to bother getting in the way or maybe he realised he'd reached the limit of his authority. Didn't matter. In the locker room, I pulled on my civvie clothes and spent a few brief minutes sorting through my field kit, pulling out the bits that I'd bought myself to supplement the crap stuff we were issued. Helmet – army's, shirt – mine. Body armour – army's, warm kit– mine. It didn't take long and then I turned, marching out of the front gate without a backwards glance.

God, that felt good!

Of course, it's the solemn duty of every has-been STAB who managed to deploy with the SF to spend the rest of their life spinning dits (stories) about their 'ally' AF tour to everyone that'll listen. And so, after a brief stop at my parent's place, I told them I'd be home later and headed out to London town. And basically, that was the next eight or so weeks. I got drunk, I gained weight, I saw old friends, I spun dits, I got in a couple of fights (and won), got mugged once (didn't win that one) and went home with what I'd like to claim was countless beautiful women but sadly I am able to remember the rather low number all too clearly.

The atmosphere in London was one of jubilation. The threat of war had hung over the city for so many months and now that it was gone, people were in their highest spirits. I began in the usual everyday bars, rubbing shoulders with office workers and tourists before I started to venture further west, signing up to a handful of the more middle-tier social clubs. Here, the clientele was a little more refined, the volume a little lower and the drinks selection a little better. This, of course, meant the hangovers were a little less and this allowed me to keep boozing. I picked up a rough crowd of regular drinking buddies, chaps who like me were jobless and directionless. Some were reservists, some had been regular soldiers and were now civilians, but it didn't matter, my parents were paying the bar tabs at this point so I was able to buy company easily.

In between bouts of raucous partying, I stared blankly at endless videos online, telling myself that the nerdy 'fact' videos were broadening my mind. After all, who doesn't want to know 'Ten best conspiracy theories ever' or 'How to memorise the names of every US President'. Honestly, the internet is a mad place.

My Dad had a word with me after a few weeks and told me in no uncertain terms that I was going to have to take it easy for a few weeks. 'Sod that!' was my first thought but the old man was right and so I decided to lay off the booze and start sweating a bit. At his suggestion, I joined the In and Out club in St James's Square which gave me the option for some late night drinking if I really fancied it but also had some excellent sports facilities and soon, I became a regular on the squash courts and in the swimming baths. Things started to improve a little.

During all this time, I'd received more than a few voicemails and texts from various people in the HAC including the Sergeant Major who was surprisingly pleasant, to the female Captain who'd fetched me from the locker room who threatened me with the Royal Military Police if I did not report to her office. Needless to say, the RMP were rather overworked at that time in Europe and had precious little time to waste chasing down a STAB who'd buggered off four days early and missed a medal parade. Still, I managed to find a telephone number for one of their Subbies and left a message explaining where to find me should they feel like arresting me. They never got back to me on that. I avoided thinking about the army. In my head, I knew I'd have to do something about it eventually but frankly, I was enjoying myself and I didn't want to have difficult conversations. The choice was taken away from me about three weeks into my membership at the In and Out club when I spied a man drinking alone at the bar.

I'd met a couple of squash chums that afternoon for a game or six and we'd retired for a gin and tonic before dinner. One of them, a retired father of two named Tom had stepped out to take a family phone call and vanished for a while. The other, a rather hatchet faced lady named Vanessa and I sat and chatted mildly over our drinks. After a few minutes she lost patience with me constantly looking across the room and demanded to know what I was ignoring her for.

"Him at the bar. The one watching everyone."

With slightly less caution than a jumbo jet taking off, Vanessa turned in her chair and eyeballed the guy for a good five second count before turning back around "What about him?"

"I reckon he's SAS."

"So? A lot of people are." Vanessa been in the Navy and retained a sailor's indifference to the dirty landlubbers in the army.

I shrugged. The guy was nondescript, plain jacket, marks and spencer tie and black brogues but every few seconds he shot a covert glance around the room and I noticed he had chosen a seat with his back to the wall, a large ornate mirror on the opposite side of the room giving him a clear view.

"Go on then, I'll bite." Vanessa sipped her drink "How do you know he's SF?"

"The way he's sat. Look at his eyes – he's watching everyone in the room. Plus he's kept his jacket buttoned whilst sitting down, maybe he's got a handgun?"

"Maybe he didn't have your HAC decorum lessons." Vanessa jibed, smiling.

At that moment, Tom returned, apologizing for his absence. He joined in the discussion but wasn't particularly interested and the subject changed as the clock ran towards dinner.

It was as I excused myself to the bathroom before we moved into the dining room that I realised the odd man at the bar was gone. Frowning, I left the room, turning towards the gents. I opened the door, stepped in and made a beeline for the urinals, passing the closed stall doors on the way. As I passed the middle, the door opened and the guy from the bar grabbed me, punched me in the stomach and slammed me back against the door. I went cross eyed as I stared down the barrel of the Glock 19 he'd drawn from a concealed holster in a movement so fast I hadn't even seen it.

"Who the eff are you and why are you following me?" he rapped out in a brutal snarl.

I wheezed as best as I could, the blow to my stomach had emptied me of air. In response, he dragged me more upright, his body turned slightly in case I moved to attack.

"Answer me." his cold eyes threatened violence.

"S – Solly!" I managed to stammer out. My heart was in my throat and I realised just how badly I'd messed up by trying to mark the guy.

"Solly what?"

"I know Solly!" I blurted out "I was with him in Europe."

"Lots of people know Solly."

"I know him! He knows me... ask him...!" it was a stupid

thing to say. How on earth was this man with his handgun still pointed at me going to ask Solly? But, to my shock he stepped back, drawing his phone from his pocket and aiming the camera at me. A few screen taps later and I heard the faint *zip* sound as he sent the image to someone. Hopefully Solly.

Seconds passed, feeling as long as hours as the Glock in his hand did not waver.

Zip

The message returned. The man with the Glock glanced at the screen and his face split into a broad grin "Alright, you're alright." The Glock was gone almost as fast as it had appeared and I breathed a sigh of relief "Solly says he knows you – says he's on his way over here too. I reckon I owe you a beer, mate?"

Suffice it to say, I learned a lesson. Not sure what the lesson was, exactly, but I learned it.

CHAPTER 6

Solly's friend was called Martin – actually that's not true. We can pretty much state that from hereon out all the names are fake for 'security reasons'. Anyway, why the hell 'Martin' was carrying that pistol with him in central London I'll never know but I'm glad he was cautious enough not to shoot me. Solly arrived about twenty minutes after our little confrontation and I apologised to Tom and Vanessa, dumping them for Solly and Martin. The three of us gathered around a table in the bar and ordered beer as Martin relayed what had just gone down between us. Solly sprayed beer foam across his lap as he snorted at the story and I tried to blush modestly but failed miserably.

Pretty soon, the beers turned into whiskies and began guiltily remembering my promise to my Dad that I'd drink less but, after all, he'd been the one to send me to this particular establishment. I promised myself that I'd work the hangover off in the gym the next day and waved for more scotch.

Solly and Martin were bloody hilarious. The collection of dits between the two of them went on for hours and I had to offer little but my enraptured attention which they drew without difficulty. The life of an SAS soldier seemed so far removed from my experience as a reservist – even including the tour I'd just finished – and I marvelled at the opportunities, experiences and as Solly put it 'bloody good fun' they'd had. Fantasies played out in my mind as I sat there of passing the arduous selection course and becoming a full time soldier.

"Oi, remember that old bloke in the bunker?" with a start, I realised Solly was addressing me. My mind flew back to Vlad and his eerie tale of the Headless valley.

"Sure. Gave me the creeps, that chap did."

"Me too! Bloody terrifying. Last thing you need when you're on ops."

"Why, what did he say?" Martin was interested now.

Solly chose that moment to begin hiccupping over his scotch, the amber liquid wobbling dangerously and so I took over the telling of Vlad's tale, butchering the dialogue and suspense, no doubt. Clearly Martin missed the point because after I'd finished speaking all he could think about was gold.

"Gold dust?" he asked, head cocked to one side "How much?"

I shrugged "I don't know. Enough for the brothers to go back. It took them weeks to paddle up the river. And plenty of others went too."

"Tons of it, I reckon." Solly had stopped hiccupping and drained his scotch, looking around for a waiter "STAB here thought he could get a bunch of the Regiment up there and we'd stop the boogie man from eating his head whilst he digs our fortune out the river." He smiled at me.

I began to make a sarcastic retort but Martin was really getting into it "Well, what about it? You say there's gold and it was what, two hundred years ago? They went up in a wooden boat with a hand sluice – surely we can do a bit better than that!"

I shook my head "It's not so wild these days, I had a quick look online when I got back. You can take a sea plane up the river and look at the falls. People canoe it all the time."

Solly looked disappointed but Martin shook his head "So? People canoeing aren't panning for gold, are they? I bet no-one's been there gold hunting for years! Besides, with a proper team and equipment we'd have a decent chance." He was really talking himself into it and – perhaps because of the scotch – he was starting to convince me.

I nodded seriously "I s'pose we could take a chopper up there and camp out for a few weeks. There must be some modern kit that sluices gold dust out of water quicker than they could."

"I know a few blokes that'd be interested." Solly interjected

"Maybe we can sign it off as adventure training?" he was grinning.

"I'm serious!" Martin protested "Look, if you're going to go, I'll come with you." he slapped his hand on my thigh in a drunken moment of emotion. Gripped by the same sense of importance, I held out my hand and we shook firmly.

"See?" I shot at Solly "We're going to be rich!"

"Or lose your heads." He wasn't taking us seriously.

"Oh, bloody hell." Martin sat back, scowling "Why'd you have to go and mention that?" he turned to me "You say you're HAC? Surely you know someone who knows about gold? Doesn't HAC stand for Have Another Chequebook?"

I affected an expression of wounded dignity and did my best to bore Martin to death with a well-rehearsed history of the Honourable Artillery Company, going back to our founding date of 25th August 1537, labouring the point that this made us the oldest *active* military corps in the world, the only older organisation being the Swiss Guard although, as a jaded looking Martin soon learned, they were not an active combat unit but rather a bodyguard-come-police force.

Hours later, I stumbled out of an overpriced black cab, bidding the driver a wonderful night and fell up the steps into my parents' house. Liberating a bottle of lager and a block of cheese from the kitchen, I snuck up to the messy room I stayed in there and planted myself in front of the ancient computer monitors that had been there since I'd written my uni dissertation. I pulled up Google and typed in 'Headless Valley'. A few sites devoted to urban legends filled the search results but a particular video from a youtuber named Mr Ballen grabbed my attention.

The legend of the Nahanni valley was as Vlad had told it. Only this video went into details that Vlad couldn't have heard. There weren't two canyons in the river, there were four and the second canyon, still known locally as Gold Creek was ten long winding miles with precious few places to land a boat safely. I'd heard the story of the three brothers from Vlad but the YouTuber put names to them: the Mcleod brothers. As it turned out, the details of all the men who'd been discovered headless in the valley were well recorded and the local police had listed all their causes of death as natural, blaming animal predation for the missing body parts.

How, I thought, could so many bodies have been found in the same state if normal animal predation were to blame? Surely there was no creature in the world that would attack a human corpse, fighting its way through the tough sinew and bone of our neck only to take the head, the toughest bone structure in the body with the least nutritious meat? No, animals would eat a body from the belly first before smaller predators came to strip away the rest of the flesh. It didn't make sense.

There were other sightings, Mr Ballen continued, strange interactions with native tribes who warned of demons and evil, glimpses through the trees of white figures, not at all like humans and one terrifying story of a man who heard small stones falling from above his camp into the river and looked up to see a naked woman, apparently feral, running on all fours up the side of a mountain.

I rolled my eyes at the stories, the gleam of Gold fading from my mind. Besides the video, there was plenty of information online about the valley, naming it as a popular tourist destination although one that only attracted the hardier kayakers and hikers. The terrain was rugged and unforgiving and did not draw the faint hearted. Nowhere, however could I find mentions of Gold, headless bodies, or modern mining operations and that sent images of yellow metal spiralling through my mind.

That was it. In my drunken state, I was completely and utterly hooked. I'd gone 'Gold mad' as they used to say in the Californian Gold rush. In my head, I sailed triumphantly down the Nahanni river, great sacks of Gold dust weighing down my boats whilst locals cheered madly. It was a wonderfully compelling image and I have to say, I'd have happily fallen asleep that night dreaming of tapping the wealth of Headless Valley but at that moment, the cheese I'd just gnawed reacted in some way with the copious amounts of Scotch I'd consumed and I spent the rest of the night curled around the toilet bowl, offering all the Gold in the world to whatever higher power would just let me stop vomiting.

CHAPTER 7

Next morning, when I was certain that it was just a hangover and I didn't need to call a mortician, I dragged my sweating carcass back to the In and Out club to burn the worst of it off. As I hammered away on the stationary bike, I couldn't shake the image of Gold from my head and Martin's words about the HAC came floating back to my head and in a momentary brainwave, I remembered a friend who'd passed the same recruits' course and now worked in the city, something big in finance. Adam, the friend, was on a few of the same WhatsApp groups I was included in despite having hung his boots up and left the reserve some years ago so I sent him a perfunctory message 'Know anything about Gold dust?'. To my surprise, he called back just a few moments later and insisted I join him for lunch. So, my mouth still tasting of peat and regret, I headed east towards Bank where Adam greeted me in a thousand pound suit, perfectly tailored to his body.

"Going up in the world?" I eyed his jacket as we shook hands.

He shrugged modestly "Money for nothing, really. I hear you've been fighting wars?"

"Oh yes, they're giving me the VC next week." I muttered sarcastically and he snorted before we settled down for an excellent meal and caught up on each other's lives.

As dessert was being served, the conversation lulled somewhat and Adam poked his glass of Sauterne across the starched white tablecloth.

"What did you mean about Gold dust?" he asked.

"Oh? Thought that'd grab your attention." I jibed.

He shot me back a grin that had little humour "Go on."

I relayed the story, a little better than I had the night before and he nodded, familiar with the story of the Mcleod brothers "Have you seen the YouTube video?" he pulled out his iPhone to show me the Mr Ballen video and I nodded enthusiastically.

"The thing is, Liam, Gold fever is no joke." He was serious "I've known a couple of chaps go off the deep end looking for the stuff. Trouble is, Gold is never found in easy places. It's either in the Americas, smothered in snakes, swamps and all sorts of nasties or it's in Africa where you're just as likely to lose your head. I know that story about the Nahanni – I think its bullshit by the way. The chances of there being Gold anywhere around there are pretty slim. It's not a wilderness anymore, there are tourists and people all over the place and no one has come back with even an ounce of the bloody metal."

Chastened, I pressed him for more details but Adam was firmly against the idea "What about a well-funded expedition?" I asked "Some of the blokes I was deployed with would be interested. If nothing else, it'd be a bloody good experience."

"A bloody expensive one, too." he scowled "I suppose you've got the cash for it though?"

"I mean – I've no idea how much something like that would cost. Nor how much we'd make if we did find something."

This was more up his street and Adam settled back, sipping the sweet wine. I eyed it jealously and he beckoned for a waiter to bring me a glass. Delicious.

"The thing is that Gold mines aren't in short supply these days. The mines in South Africa alone supply enough for most of the western world. But the good thing about it is gold is always stable. It rarely loses its value and that's why it's still a big thing in trading."

"How much could you make from panning?" I asked.

Adam shook his head "Panning is what they did in the old days and you still get some hobbyists doing it now. All panning does though is give you an indication that there's a lot of gold in the area. Then you search for the vein and you mine it."

I frowned, confused "But the Mcleod brothers weren't there

with pickaxes were they?" in my mind, the three brothers had stood in the shallows, scooping gold flakes out of the water and piling it into a small mountain of shiny metal next to them. But Adam was shaking his head.

"No. Like I say, panning just indicates there is a gold vein. I can't remember if the Mcleods found a mine or they were sluicing it." He stared at the table for a moment, thinking "No, they must have been sluicing it. Three men wouldn't make a lot of headway digging in that spot. But-"

"What's sluicing?" I interrupted.

"Ah – it's more or less what it sounds like. In the gold rush days, there were a lot of bright minds trying to find the quickest and cheapest ways to extract gold. Remember, in California it was a mad, every man for himself type of rush. There weren't huge corporations vying for control of an entire mine and shipping in machines and workforces. This was the average Adam –" he smiled as he tapped his own chest "- trying to fill his saddlebags. Nothing more. So the sluices were a type of filter box they'd put in the stream and the gold dust would settle in it."

"But how did the filters work? Is the gold just floating around? Wouldn't it just wash away?" my mind was buzzing with questions.

Adam was patient "No. Actually, I've not explained it that well. Bear in mind that I've never done this, I've just heard it described." He sipped his wine as he thought it through "Take our average Adam again. He's panned in a river and found some flecks of dust so, he gets a bucket and digs some of the sediment out of the river."

"Sediment? What if the riverbed is rocky?" I thought back to mountain streams I'd seen on holidays in the Pyrenees as a child.

"No, you wouldn't bother panning there. The gold is in the sediment because the water has crushed the surrounding rocks and that's how the flakes come loose."

"Right. So you've got a bucket full of mud –"

"Sediment. A bucket full of sediment. Then you set the sluice down in the water where the flow is strong but not strong enough to wash your sluice away. I think they weight it down with a rock or something – I don't know. But you get the picture, right?"

"Right. And the sluice is a sort of filter?" I asked.

"Exactly. So, you take your bucket of sediment and you tip it into the sluice. Then, the flowing water washes it through the filters which let the smaller particles of rock through but hold the gold dust."

"So, they don't need to like, crank a handle or something?"

Adam laughed "No! Like I said, it's supposed to be easy. One bloke can do it by himself."

I thought about it, Gold firmly back in my mind.

Adam brought me back down to earth "It's a crap way to make money in the modern day, Liam. You'd be there for months, eating terrible food, looking over your shoulder for bears and wolves and more than likely, dying of exposure."

"Right. That's why I want to take the SAS with me."

Adam rolled his eyes "Oh, bloody hell. Liam, I'm serious. People go nuts looking for gold. It's not the money maker you think it is."

"But surely if you find enough then it's a good return?"

He rolled his eyes "Yeah, yeah. I know what you mean." a deep sigh "The biggest nugget ever found is called the Mojave nugget and a prospector found it in the sixties or seventies – I can't remember which. It weighs about four or five kilos and everyone who talks about gold uses it as an example of how you can strike it rich. It's BS. You've got more chance of winning the lottery these days than you have of making a fortune gold panning."

Adam was resolute. He told me stories of people in his company who'd caught gold fever. One, a colleague he'd known well had vanished in the Amazon chasing down a vague rumour of golden walled temples. Another, a father of three had emptied his bank account and sold his house in an ill informed bid to claim the yellow metal from a sunken Roman ship in the Mediterranean and had gone bankrupt as a result. His wife had left him and he'd been sectioned and was now in an institution.

"Look, mate." I pleaded with Adam "I'm not about to go off half cocked. Maybe there is gold there, maybe there isn't but the whole thing sounds bloody good fun!"

Adam rolled his eyes "Why don't you just go out there on holiday? I think you can canoe the river – it sounds like a barrel of fun! When you get there, you'll see there's no gold and that'll be it! Do that before you waste your cash on some suicide quest."

That wasn't what I wanted and he knew it. But Adam was deadly serious. I could see why he was concerned but in my head, the risk was negligible. If nothing else, I thought, I'd have a cracking time in the wild with my mates from the SAS and if we came back empty handed? Oh well. We'd have the memory at least!

Adam and I parted ways, he back to the office and I to wander aimlessly down London streets. An hour or so later, Adam pinged me a text which stopped me in my tracks.

Look, you're stubborn enough to go and do this whatever I tell you so IF you decide to go to the Nahanni (and I stress, DON'T) then I know a chap named Johannes de Villiers who went gold mad. He's about as professional as you can get in gold exploration but he's a complete headcase. You'll get along well. Anyway, I'll send him your number and IF you go into the Nahanni valley, take him with you.

I hastened to reply my thanks but Adam was not appeased.

If you die in Headless Valley, just remember I bloody well told you so. You and Johannes deserve each other.

Oh, and if you do strike it rich. Give me a call. I'll turn the gold into money for you.

Which, I reasoned, was my friend's way of telling me to watch my back.

CHAPTER 8

Johannes de Villiers was a thin, wiry looking middle aged white man who could have teleported into London from the bush a second before. A weeks' worth of greying stubble covered his chin and cheeks, his eyes constantly twitched at small movements and if a smile had ever cracked his tombstone features, I'd eat the dirty, sweat stained leather cowboy hat that perched on his greasy locks.

We met at Adam's invitation in a small but exclusive restaurant tucked around the side of Bank. I was early and the staff wouldn't let me in until Adam arrived, precisely five minutes before our reservation time. Annoyed at being made to stand in the street, I didn't bother to conceal my disgust at the ragged, pound-shop version of Crocodile Dundee that Adam had dragged with him.

"Liam, Johannes – Johannes, Liam."

I held out my hand and Johannes looked surprised but took it in a limp grip, releasing it almost at once. His hands were calloused and the nails on each finger were bitten down to the quick. Adam seemed to be repressing a smile at my reaction and I resisted the urge to shoot him a scathing look.

We sat down at crisp white linen as the waiters poured overpriced red wine and Adam exchanged small pleasantries. Johannes looked so out of place he may as well have been a wild animal, his appearance so at odds with the business or smart casual attire the few other diners sported.

"Johannes has just got back from a trip in Madagascar." Adam was saying. He looked at the South African expectantly.

"Yeh."

I held a moment's amused looked with Adam.

"I thought Madagascar was mostly a wildlife reserve?" I pressed.

"Is." was the laconic reply "No harm in looking though, huh? When you planning to leave?"

I blinked in astonishment "Leave?"

"For the Nahanni? Boss –" he indicated Adam "- says you got gold fever. Strike whilst the stone's burning." He sat back in the leather bound chair and let out a heaving wheeze which after I'd frantically cast around for a paramedic or a defibrillator, I realised was the bushman's laugh. Apparently, this was his idea of a joke.

"Well, we hadn't even got as far as what we'd actually need..."

Johannes became all business at once "We'd need ten men, no less. Three boats to get up the river, rifles at least for every man, three months food minimum, a rescue team back in Fort Simpson..." the list went on. I wondered if I was supposed to be taking notes.

"We hadn't actually decided to go yet." I protested.

Adam held up his hands "For the record, I am *not* going. And I still don't think you should but Johannes is the man to take if you are going."

"Boss says you know some guys in the S-A-S?" he spaced the acronym out, overpronouncing each syllable as though it were an unfamiliar term.

"Right. I – look, have you been there?"

"No. Been to the northwest territories though. Tough ground, that. Need tough guys with you. I can sort most of the equipment in country. Need airline tickets, visas and in-date passports. You got the cash?"

"Cash?" I was lost in Johannes' whirlwind pace.

Adam cleared his throat "Johannes is a freelancer and he doesn't fund expeditions out of his own pocket. What he's asking is can you fund the expedition?"

"I –" I stuttered. My own bank account was as empty as ever.

I was living with my parents, spending from their credit cards. Of course, the family were never short of a bob or two but this sounded expensive.

"I thought you were ready to go?" Johannes looked annoyed.

"Are you?" Adam flipped the responsibility for answering to me.

"I- "

"What you waiting for? Book the tickets and we'll go." Johannes seemed ready to leave there and then.

I tried to frame an argument: I didn't have the money lined up, let alone a cost schedule but Adam was looking smug and self-satisfied and suddenly, I was fed up.

"Alright." I nodded.

"Alright?" Adam's eyes were wide with shock.

"Alright!" I declared. Johannes nodded as though this was a foregone conclusion and then turned expectantly to the waiter who arrived with his lunch which he devoured, paying no further attention to Adam or I.

"Liam –" Adam began but I cut him off.

"No! I've had enough. Enough pissing my life away in London doing nothing. Look, I hardly need the money, you know that but I do need an adventure. It doesn't matter if we find the gold or not –" Johannes froze and I hastily corrected myself "- but we'll find it. I know we will."

Adam rolled his eyes but he'd already voiced his protests. He'd set the ball rolling and now that the decision was made, he began to chatter about the finer details.

"Now, because the dust you sluice won't be totally pure, I think we'll aim for a sale price of forty five thousand pounds per kilo. With ten of you, you'll need to get about forty kilos worth which should hit a sale price –" Adam paused to scribble on a napkin "one point eight million pounds. Split ten ways, that's-"

"One hundred and eighty grand." I nodded "That's a lot of money."

"Kit costs money." Johannes interjected, a spot of brown joux caught in his chin stubble.

I happily disregarded his words, a swell of elation rising in me. I couldn't keep the grin off my face as Johannes began to talk about boats and food supplies. I was suddenly struck by the sight of this rough outdoorsman in the posh London setting and it occurred to me how many of the legendary explorers of old, Shackleton, Scott, Cook, Drake and countless others had started their adventure in this exact setting, probably down to the crisp white napkins and Beaujolais. Adam caught my expression and asked what was on my mind. I told him and he, the selfish swine had to spoil the moment.

"Scott froze to death, remember and Cook was lynched by natives."

I started to argue but Johannes loudly interrupted our bickering by asking who was coming with us. I gave him a brief overview of Solly, Martin and our drunken discussion. Johannes would talk no further until I'd rung Solly and so I dialled his number. To my surprise, Johannes rested his ear against the back of my phone to listen.

I ran Solly through it and he grunted several times in response. I half expected him to rubbish the idea but instead he gave a terse "I'll make some calls" and hung up. I shrugged at Johannes.

Adam had ordered a second bottle of wine and his sourness had evaporated, leading him to cajole Johannes into detailing what we'd need.

"Ten blokes. No less."

"Why ten?"

"Multiple boats, more bodies to carry kit, keep watch at night and enough faces to hide behind if we don't get on."

In my mind's eye, we crouched on the river bank in the shade of the trees, stacks of gold piled up around us.

"You'll need a sluice." Adam pointed out.

"How much do the boxes cost?" I wondered.

Johannes and Adam paused for a moment before baying with laughter "We don't sluice for gold, man!" Johannes cackled "It's not eighteen hundred anymore!"

I blinked at their amusement "How am I supposed to know that?"

"Coz, man! You're going into the Headless Valley to find gold! What'cha think, we'd be up to our knees in the river? Christ!" Johannes was wheezing so hard he had to stop speaking.

"Alright, alright! You've had your fun. What do we use?" I demanded, not a little put out at being the butt of the joke.

"Most common is a high banker –" Adam began but Johannes, wiping away a tear, cut him off.

"We need the X Flare."

Adam looked pained "Those are hard to come by."

"Not a bloody option. No X Flare, no point."

"What's an –"

"It's an experimental machine for gold extraction." Adam had actually lowered his voice "The reason it's a bit suspect, is the Chinese Government seized them off a group of illegal miners they caught. According to the CCP, they're the ones that came up with the idea and trying to get hold of one means dealing with them directly."

"Commie or Capitalist, who cares! Get the damn machine." Johannes declared, rapping the table with a knuckle.

"Can you get it?" I asked Adam and he nodded slowly.

"Probably. It'll be forty or fifty grand though."

I was crestfallen. That was nearly half my share of the potential profits plus the fact that I'd have to front the cost of the boats and other equipment we'd need. Not to mention the airline tickets. Johannes was already shaking his head.

"See, boss, this isn't a one off. We strike gold in the Nahanni, we head back again and again. Once you find the gold, that's just the start. You break even this trip, maybe next trip we have bigger boats and you come back a millionaire." he grinned yellow teeth at me "Think about the long term, boss."

I thought about it. I thought about it a lot more that evening when I broached the subject to my parents. Surprisingly, they were interested in the scheme (it helped that I made no mention of bodies found with missing heads nor mysteriously vanishing tribes of Indians) and agreed to front some of the cost on the basis that I pay them back from the profits. But the real kicker was when Solly rang me back at midnight to say he'd got eight SAS blokes, himself included and they'd managed to pass the whole expedition off as a training exercise so would supply their own kit. There were still one or two items I'd need to provide and the tickets across the Atlantic, but otherwise, we were go!

CHAPTER 9

"I thought it was summer?" I didn't bother to keep the grumble from my tone as I shivered in the supposedly 'warm' weather.

Johannes gave his bark of a laugh "Colder than Madagascar!" he dissolved into the heart attack convulsions that for him qualified as a laugh.

I stared out over the windswept tarmac of the single runway that served Fort Simpson airport. All around, the trees that covered most of this region were held back by the neatly trimmed grass lining the concrete. A number of small aircraft were dotted around the sleepy airport, most making a living off of tourist or sightseeing flights. A small café held the few living souls within the boundaries of the facility and as I stared through the glass at the warm interior, I hoped the air traffic controllers had remained at their post as the dark dot Johannes and I watched on the horizon materialised into a chunky looking propellor driven cargo plane.

"Here they come." Johannes pointed out unnecessarily and as a bearded local with a dirty baseball cap stepped out of the café to smoke I pointed at the approaching aircraft and he glanced once at it before shrugging nonchalantly.

"Bloody hell." I muttered watching the flaps set on the wings as the pilots made their final approach.

"You worry too much, boss." despite being at least two decades my senior and vastly more experienced, Johannes had happily deferred to my command in the planning of our expedition. This meant that the past four weeks that I'd 'lived' in

Fort Simpson had been amongst the busiest of my life. Solly and his chaps had a very specific window of opportunity to be away from their jobs and so I'd had to organise everything myself, more or less draining all the funds I'd budgeted for the trip.

"I worry because it's my neck on the line if they crash into the runway." I grumbled but in truth, I was almost shaking with excitement at the arrival of Solly and the final equipment shipment he was bringing.

"All our necks when we're upriver." Johannes replied in a rare sober moment "Specially if those boats are crap, eh?"

I ground my teeth. The three boats I'd managed to purchase after a great deal of tedious research and phone calls to some extremely dull people, were Rigid Raiders, a type commonly in use by the Royal Marines and I knew at least two of Solly's guys were well versed in their use. In the interests of time, we'd agreed a morning to familiarise ourselves with their function followed by a slow first afternoon upriver to practice our piloting skills.

The boats were not crap, although at £3000 each they were a steal. I'd been assured that this low price did not affect their quality but I was still annoyed a having to use such a pedestrian mode of transport.

"Why can't we take a Land Cruiser again?" I asked as the aircraft's tyres squeaked on the runway and the engines went into reverse thrust.

"Too rugged." Johannes snapped "Can't drive into the wilderness. S'not the outback. Besides, you like Land Rovers!"

"If you want to go into the outback, take a Land Rover." I quoted "But if you want to come back –"

"Bring a Land Cruiser." Johannes finished, chuckling "Not getting there on four wheels, boss. Can't go landing a plane in that canyon either."

"Maybe we should've landed on top of the cliffs?" I wondered suddenly "Abseiled down?"

He looked askance "All that way? That's a lot of rope. Then you've got to get back up. And think about all them caves! No,

Boss! No climbing on the rocks. We stay on the water and on the shore. Got those rifles for whatever we find in the caves."

If the boats had been cheap, the weapons I'd bought were not. Solly had insisted on a veritable arsenal, even going so far as to find a contact who could bring the weapons to a rendezvous on the river. When I'd questioned the legality of such a move he'd grunted down the phone at me, telling me that such trivialities didn't matter in the rural territories. So, we were planning on meeting some shady Canadian further up the river who would provide us with enough weaponry to fight a small war. He'd even buy the guns back from us after the expedition was done, a fact that had done little to persuade me of his reliability. Still, Solly was adamant and the cash now sat in a waterproof box in the back of the truck I'd hired.

"Is that him?" Johannes pointed as the propellors came to a stop and a squat figure made his way down to the tarmac, stretching in the sun. I nodded and led the way across to the aircraft, ignoring the staring faces in the café.

"Solly!"

"Good to see you, pal!" Solly was fairly buzzing with enthusiasm, turning to introduce the seven others he'd managed to persuade "You know Martin and Doug –" we shook hands with a grin "This is Colin, Andy, Robbie and Jeff."

Those four were younger, about my own age and gave waves as they busied themselves removing the three boats from the back of the cargo plane.

A final man, the eighth of the SAS chaps was still in the back of the hold, moving around some crates of kit that had doubtless cost me a small fortune. Solly beckoned him out and I almost fell over as striding down the ramp came the ugly, miserable form of Gibbo, my former PSI.

"Stryker." he grimaced, holding out an unwilling hand.

"Gibbo." I tried to keep my features peaceable. What was Solly playing at bringing him along?

"You know each other?" he asked in surprise.

"Oh, we goes way back." Gibbo was smiling now "One of my

little berks when I was PSI."

Solly gave a slow nod. I could tell he was annoyed that he hadn't know this but I also knew that he'd handpicked every man for a specific skillset. I wondered if Gibbo's was going to be abusing the head-eating monsters we might encounter.

"Boats all good, Sol." The soldier named Andy had approached and took a moment to elbow Gibbo aside, shaking my hand warmly "Good to meet you, mate. Looking forward to this!"

The others were similarly friendly. It was an odd group. Most of the men were fairly quiet, speaking only when necessary or when the odd snatch of banter presented itself. All apart from Jeff who was easily Johannes' age or older but moved with the ease of a far younger man. He still bore the tattoo of the Parachute Regiment on his right bicep (permanently exposed to the elements) and immediately began to poke fun at my Spec Inf background which I responded to in turn and we got on famously.

I introduced Johannes which went down about as well as a lead balloon. The Afrikaner was dour and uninterested, seeming only to think of getting on the river and barely helping as we loaded the boats onto a flatbed which headed back into town as I drove a pickup with Solly, Johannes and Doug.

"Sorry about Gibbo." Solly called from the back seat "I know he's a prick but he's been all over the northwest territories. Couldn't find another bloke who had the experience. Try not to worry about him too much."

It didn't bring a warm fuzzy feeling to my head but Johannes was quick to dismiss my concerns "That's why we've got ten, boss. More faces to hide behind."

"He's right." Doug, the Scottish soldier I'd met in Europe piped up "Team this size is just right to maintain for a couple of months. They send ten man teams to the arctic for research."

I shrugged but Johannes was already talking again.

"Could get on the water this afternoon, boss?"

"You're chomping at the bit." I grumbled but Solly agreed there was no reason to wait and that afternoon we got the three craft on the water and under the close instruction of Robbie and Colin, we learned the basics of piloting the rugged boats upriver. As the light began to fail, we busied ourselves with the gear we'd need to survive for the next few months. Johannes, I noticed seemed to shirk most of the work, instead examining the X Flare, the hi-tech sluicing machine we'd bought.

"Is it alright?" I approached him, intending to press him into service carrying some of the heavier crates of dried food that Solly was dragging down to the water.

"All good." Johannes didn't even blink as he stared at the complex looking machinery. It was like he'd discovered some religious artefact and I remembered Adam's warnings about the South African being gold mad.

"It doesn't look very big." I observed.

He snickered "Don't need to be. Most efficient sluicing kit the world's ever seen." He glanced at me and I saw the red veins in the whites of his eyeballs "Something like this is what us in the gold world have been waiting for. Trust the Chinamen to come up with it."

Sensing xenophobia, I fell back on my Britishness and made an excuse to get away from the grizzled prospector. Solly pulled me aside for a quiet word.

"Your saffa –" he nodded towards the enthralled Johannes "- is he all there?"

"Not even a little bit." I smiled to show I wasn't worried "But we need him as much as we need anyone on this. He's the gold man. He's done this before and nobody died."

"There's always a first time." Solly looked genuinely concerned and I'll admit, it annoyed me. I'd spent months now planning this, dished out thousands of pounds that I now owed to my parents and shivered my balls off in this godforsaken outpost of civilisation waiting for Solly to show up and I didn't like him questioning my decision making. I told him so, too and he turned with raised eyebrows.

"Steady on, old chap."

I shrugged "Johannes is as much an issue as Gibbo."

Solly rolled his eyes "Gibbo isn't all bad."

I relayed my story from recruits of Thompson punching the bullying Sergeant and Solly nodded, knowingly.

"We knew that when he came through training wing. Thing is, Liam I think the Regiment has been good for him. Despite what you think he's a good soldier and a sterling bloke under fire. I think when he was around you in the HAC he was the wrong bloke in the wrong place. He wanted more from his job and instead they sent him there for two years and then made him a Colour Sergeant. He didn't want that so he got himself fit and came to us. Now he's happier and all that crap with the recruits doesn't cut any ice with us. He's gone from being a big fish lost in a big pond to a small fish in a very small pond."

"He's a wanker."

Solly snorted "You're probably not wrong, mate. But give him a chance, yeah? It's going to be a long trip if you're already on the wrong foot."

"Same as you with Johannes." I pointed out.

"Yeah, yeah. Look, he's right that having a crowd of us makes it easier to avoid one another if we need to but when we get there we're probably going to have days where there's only one or two of us in the camp."

I regarded him suspiciously "What's your point?"

Solly sighed "Just keep an eye on him for me and I'll keep Gibbo under control."

I shrugged and Solly clapped me on the arm, turning to supervise the rest of the kit loading.

As we set off upriver, finally leaving the bland grey buildings of Fort Simpson behind us I breathed a sigh of relief, the stress of the past few weeks now rapidly turning to excitement. I looked around at the grizzled and tough faces on the boat with me, nodding at the kit that Solly's blokes were wearing. I'd dared to ask Solly why we needed body armour but he'd sniggered saying he and his blokes didn't go many places without it. Still, everything the SAS had brought with them was of the highest quality and Johannes, for all his weirdness was the best in his field. All in all, I fancied our chances of success in the Headless Valley were pretty high. All we needed now was for the river to release its bounty.

And that was out of my control.

CHAPTER 10

Solly's rendezvous was planned a safe distance from prying eyes in the town. To my surprise, he was chattering on a satellite phone as we cruised up the wide, meandering length of the Liard river that would eventually lead us to the Nahanni. To the south, I knew a small road ran almost parallel to the water although the thick trees on the bank obscured it from our view. Solly had the boats stop several times whilst he held muttered conversations with his contact and peered intently at a GPS before his face deepened in a frown of consternation.

"Bloody officers can never navigate." Martin grumbled from the pilot's chair. I was crouched beside him, wondering what I'd do if I started getting seasick and I snorted at the comment.

"Thought he used to be a Sergeant?"

"He did, but at Sandhurst they make you forget common sense, remember?" Martin sniggered, referencing the army's officer training school. Solly shot us a filthy look, directing Martin to pull into a sandy cove with driftwood lining the shore.

Waiting for us was a nondescript removal truck with the fading letters of the company name printed on the sides. The driver was one of the most carefully bland men I'd ever met, average height, average build, slightly too long hair, stubble, and a dull, disinterested expression on his face.

Solly shook hands with him and he opened the tailgate of the truck to reveal crates of rifles, handguns and (to my shock) grenades.

"Are we fighting a war? I thought you said a bit of sport shooting?" I demanded of Solly and he looked serious for a moment.

"Remember I signed this off as adventurous training?" he reminded me and I shrugged,

"Thought that meant hiking and climbing?"

"Not in the Regiment." He explained "Woods out here are as good a place as any to get some shooting done. It'll be good training for us all, keep our minds busy if the gold isn't – ah - forthcoming."

It seemed overkill but I had to admit as the professionally stoic special forces men turned into whooping schoolboys at the sight of all the 'fun stuff', that blowing up a few trees for the next few months was likely to be a hobby I'd enjoy. Still, the boats were now heavier than ever although Martin reminded me we could always spend a day burning through all the ammo if we needed to.

"Sounds like my type of fun." he grinned, shoving the throttle open and pushing the boat out into mid-stream.

I was annoyed, I'll admit but something I hadn't factored into this trip was establishing a clear chain of command. Clearly, Solly was used to being in charge and during our time in Europe that had been the arrangement. He also outranked all of us in the army and despite my lack of attendance, I was still a serving soldier. But we weren't in uniform here and it was both my idea, organisation and funding that had brought us to the wilds of Canada and although I'm not the type to throw my weight around micromanaging people, I felt a surge of near panic at the idea that I was losing control of the expedition. Part of the problem was that the SAS guys were intimidating. Sure, I knew Doug, Martin and Solly fairly well by now but they listened to each other and knew their business, particularly when it came to the thousand small details of administration that came with surviving out here. They weren't looking to me for instruction and Solly was navigating us with his expensive GPS. There was also the fact that I was the only 'unskilled' labour aboard the boats. Solly was the leader, Gibbo knew the wilderness, Johannes was the gold expert and the others were useful muscle with a dozen tours under their belts whereas I, even after my hours at the In and Out club gym couldn't even really be said to qualify as 'muscle'.

In any case, my insecurities didn't affect our journey as we slowed for the night and set about the laborious task of making camp on the riverbank. Fortunately, the weather was kind to us and we passed our first night without incident although as always when I slept under the stars I woke a hundred times during the night and shivered my way through the small hours in my sleeping bag.

Once the unpleasantness of wilderness toileting was complete, we breakfasted on a well rationed supply of mixed dried and fresh food which we would soon try to supplement by hunting and fishing in the canyon. We had plenty of food and supplies but it made sense to preserve it as much as possible and I was looking forward to shedding the last of the weight I'd gained post-deployment.

Or so I told my growling stomach as we set off again.

With several false starts spotting offshoots of the river that turned out to be misleading oxbow lakes we finally approached the small settlement of Nahanni Butte which marked the entrance to the river. From here, our spirits picked up and there were ribald comments echoing from the water between the boats as the three craft drew abreast and began to race one another, much to our amusement. However, there were still long days of travel ahead and the mood quickly dampened as the seemingly endless sights of passing trees, local wildlife and distant mountains began to lose their splendour.

"Be quicker on the way back!" Martin called from the bows as I took my turn piloting the craft. I shot him the finger in response provoking a cackle of laughter before I wobbled the controls, forcing him to grab the side of the boat to steady himself.

"You cheeky –" he began, rounding on me with mock vengeance but Solly gave a shout and I looked up to see a small group of men standing beside the river, clearly beckoning for us to stop. Instinctively, I eased the throttle back, holding the wheel steady as the boat began to bob in the current. Gibbo was shouting something from the next boat and Solly apparently heard him although I couldn't make out a word.

"Pull over on the beach, Liam." Solly ordered and I nosed the shallow craft onto land.

The group of three were clearly natives by their appearance, perhaps hunters because they had serious looking rifles over their shoulders and heavy packs. They had the dour expressions that I'd come to associate with the older First Nations people in the region and if they were surprised to see us, they hid it well.

Introductions were made as Solly, Johannes and I greeted them. Their names were Bineshii, Niimi and John. I blinked at the last name but apparently no-one else thought it odd as the men explained they were part of a small community trying to live in the wilds of the Nahanni, reclaiming a way of semi-nomadic life their ancestors had lived before the western settlers came.

We didn't mention gold. Instead, we gave the excuse that we were soldiers on a training exercise with the authority of the Canadian government which wasn't strictly untrue – Solly had contacted one of his opposite numbers in the Canadian special forces who had greenlit the operation and smoothed over a lot of the more political details.

Gibbo came ashore and gave a friendly greeting in a native language which provoked the first warm expression on the men's faces. Thereafter, their attitude improved considerably and we ended up chatting for some time as I grudgingly admitted to myself that perhaps Gibbo was of some use after all. Solly had eyed up the hunting rifles the men carried and soon arranged for a small box of ammunition to be distributed amongst them following Gibbo's explanation that gift giving was a common courtesy amongst visitors to native lands. This was readily received and the brass rounds vanished into pouches and pockets with a speed I'd not have thought the men capable of. In return, we were handed a pouch of rough cut tobacco which they explained was to be given as an offering to the river when we reached the canyons.

"We'll come with you." Bill announced suddenly.

Instinctively, I rejected the idea not wanting to spread the word of our gold seeking quest. But Solly caught my eye and shrugged, the small movement hefting the rifle he had slung over his shoulder and I considered briefly. Here we were, a small army in the wilderness and they were three older natives trying to reclaim a lost sense of the past. I guessed that gold in the quantities we were planning on retrieving was about as useful to them as a punch in the throat.

Johannes pulled me aside as Solly and Gibbo chatted to the men. He hissed at me in his clipped Afrikaner tones "Hey, boss, we don't need them. They're just here to sniff out the gold and I'll betcha they scoot the moment we find anything yellow." he was as serious as I'd ever seen the man, a frantic energy in his eyes.

"They're just going to guide us in." I pointed out.

"Guide?" he spat "It's a straight river, boss. We've got GPS, maps, and compass. I can guide us from here even if you cut out my eyes!" at this he drew a knife from beneath his shirt and held it up to his wide eyes as though he meant to gouge them out there on the riverbank.

Wide eyed myself, I hastened to push his hand down and he reluctantly lowered the blade back to the hidden sheath.

"Look, there's only two of them and –"

"There's more than two, boss! There'll be a hundred of them or more, all armed!"

A fit of frustration, no doubt inspired by the tedious days on the river gripped me "Look, we're surrounded by the SAS and they're all armed to the teeth, every one of them! No-one – no matter how many of them are getting through this lot! Let them see we're gathering gold. They don't have the X Flare nor the boats to transport it. There is literally zero chance of them stealing it."

He stared at me with his wide eyed madness. The man was bonkers – there was no denying it but he seemed to see the logic in my argument, turning his head and spitting which I took to mean a reluctant consent but as I turned away, he muttered under his breath "… never asked *what* all those guns are for."

Rolling my eyes, I invited the three men aboard. Bineshii declined, melting away into the trees as his two friends joined our boat and we resumed our trip.

As it turned out, the two natives quickly earned their place pointing out the slacker water at each stage of the river and directing us so that we made far better time that we had thus far. They supervised the offering of tobacco to the river as we approached the thick sulphur stench of the Kraus hot springs, marking the next major landmark on our quest. To my surprise, Gibbo watched this superstitious rite with something approaching reverence and quickly snarled at any sceptical voices that were raised. He'd moved over to our boat, relegating Martin to the craft behind us and chattered with our two guides as I took my turn piloting and guided us up the channels they pointed out as we entered the gloomy rock lined walls of First Canyon.

We knew from our preparations that First Canyon had nowhere for us to land, being comprised solely of cave filled rocks on either side. I pointed this out to our two guides who nodded sagely, advising us to run out our riding lights.

"It's always dark in the canyon." John told me in his deep, halting voice "Doesn't matter if its night or day."

"Will we make it to Second Canyon by tonight?" I asked with not a little concern. I'd not planned on spending the night travelling.

"No problem." John nodded "Be later on but we'll get there."

Although the light was fading slowly into a long dusk, on the water we had to switch on the powerful floodlights. The electric beams allowed us to navigate easily but they also served to turn the water to an impenetrable black surface, looking ever more sinister as the evening drew on.

Solly tossed me a strip of jerky to chew as I piloted, backing the throttle off as the water began to churn ahead.

"Are there rapids?" I asked and the guides nodded. That was fine, I'd planned for that and this was one of the reasons we'd chosen these boats. However, reading about the theory of piloting a boat up a rapid and actually doing it safely were wildly different and in the gleam of the floodlights I could see my knuckles turning white on the hard polymer of the steering wheel.

We made it through the length of First Canyon safely although by the time we emerged onto the small open stretch of river that led to our destination, night had fallen. Before we'd left, I'd been looking forward to a few of the more spectacular sights specifically hoping to lay eyes on the aurora borealis, the northern lights. But now, as I steered us towards what I hoped was a dry bed for the evening I was struck by how black the sky looked. At no point in the stygian blanket of the heavens did a star or planet glimmer for us to see. Perhaps it was the brilliance of our own artificial light that blocked my sight but with the dark liquid below us, the immense rock faces on either side and the impenetrable blackness above, I started to long for bright sunshine and mentally recalled images of sandy beaches.

"Look out!" Gibbo was in the bows and he snapped at me, pointing out a stream of white water we were fast approaching. I cursed, knowing that if he'd not been blocking my view, I'd have seen the rapid earlier but now we were on the wrong side of the river and our guides had gone very still, staring at the danger ahead.

With a shaking sound, the boat struck the white water and I immediately twisted the wheel as I'd been told, fighting the force of the water that threatened to turn our nose back downstream. Solly crouched next to me, lowering himself in the small boat to maintain his balance and I could feel the palpable tension coming off of him.

"Rocks!" Gibbo bawled, moving across my field of vision to point and I snarled at him to move his useless carcass out of the way and turned the wheel but with a grinding crash, I felt the keel strike something solid.

Frantically, I tried to turn away as Gibbo wobbled dangerously in the bows but the current was strong and the impact had slowed us and the river immediately struck, spinning the nose of the boat hard to my left.

I rammed the throttle forward, hearing a shout of alarm from the other boats and wrenched the wheel to try and recover our position and face back upstream but another hard impact, perhaps the same rock we'd already struck and the boat tilted sickeningly sideways and I just had time to see Gibbo lose his grip and tumble overboard before a bone jarring jolt lifted me from my seat and sent me crashing into the icy black surface of the Nahanni.

CHAPTER 11

I felt every muscle clench and a futile protest leave my lips as I struck the surface. I'd braced myself for the cold but as I tumbled in the water, it was the sudden, agonising pain in my leg that dulled every other sense. The water could have been made of ice for all the heed I paid it. Instead, the second my head was clear of the surface I let loose a blood curling shriek of pounding agony.

My right leg from the knee downwards felt as though the bone itself had been laid open from end to end. White fire burned beneath the skin and I instinctively reached down to cup the limb, my head falling back below the surface.

I inhaled water. The first kiss in my passionate relationship with the Nahanni.

I need to breathe

My scream had sacrificed the little air I'd retained in my lungs and now the river was driving me down into its depths. Something hard struck my head and I saw flashing lights in front of my vision as my chest began to burn for oxygen.

Gold

Surely that was flakes of the elusive metal floating before me? I swiped my hand through the image, the agony in my lower body forgotten for a second and it vanished like a fleeting daydream.

CRACK

My head struck the solid surface again and I realised the river had thrown me against a rock. Frantically, I clawed my way up its rough edge, thanking whatever fluke of nature that had cast the boulder into the depths below and then my head broke the surface and bright light dazzled me and I coughed and spluttered like shipwrecked sailor.

Rough hands were grabbing me and I managed to choke out that my leg was broken but they hauled me over the side of the boat all the same and dumped me roughly on the floor where I clamped my jaw shut against the scream, now letting out a weird, muted animalistic moan which stopped the rough hands trying to strip my wet clothes from my body.

"Which leg?" someone snapped and I choked out that it was my right.

"Arms up." my shirt and jacket were gone, a second later someone was wrapping a foil survival blanket around me and asking me if I was hurt anywhere else.

"Just the leg."

"Your head's bleeding, fella."

"The rocks."

"Saved your life. Lucky your skull's so thick, eh?"

I opened my eyes to see Jeff, the oldest man on the expedition looking down at me with raised eyebrows. By my feet, Doug was slicing through my trouser leg with medical shears. I tried to protest and he looked directly at me, paused and then flicked me in the leg.

I bit my tongue so hard that blood filled my mouth as I writhed and thrashed.

"Broken." he called over the sound of the engine. Were we still moving?

"No shit." Jeff agreed.

"How you feeling, Stryker?"

I let out a series of heavy breaths, trying to calm my racing mind and clear the shock from my head "Cold."

"Wrap him up. Here, have a nibble on this."

There was the sound of plastic being unwrapped and then a sweet, slightly pungent taste as a lollipop was shoved into my cheek. I sucked greedily on the sweet, willing its magic properties to take effect.

Fentanyl.

A name in some parts of the world synonymous with corrupt doctors, addiction, and degradation. The lozenge I was sucking on was the standard battlefield painkiller, used for anything from gunshot wounds to severed limbs. Within a couple of minutes, I could feel the effects as the agony in my leg faded to a dull burning sensation.

"Alright?"

"Very." I was high as kite. Despite everything, I was smiling "Is Gibbo alright?"

"Is Gibbo ever alright?" Jeff answered. I'd learned that he never answered a question straight. There was always a joke. I wondered vaguely if he did this under fire or if this version of the grey haired man was what compensated for his abilities as an operator "He's wet and miserable. Bit like his wife."

I snorted and nearly choked on the lozenge which was nearly gone. That made my leg move which sent pain burning through me again.

Jeff looked around "Think we're here."

"Second Canyon?" I asked and he nodded.

"One after first."

"Stop here!" I heard Solly's voice shouting, echoing off the walls of rock that were invisible to me from my prone position oin the bottom of the Raider.

"Right, Liam? We're going to have to get you out of the boat." Doug's Scottish tones were reassuring but I felt my muscles tense with anticipation "We'll use this as a stretcher – hang on."

He vanished from view. The boat had stopped moving although I could still hear the river rushing besides us. Voices were calling orders on the shore and I had a sensation of people moving around on a rocky beach.

"Here." Doug was back with a long sheet of black material which was rigid, about four feet long,

"That's off the X Flare!" I gasped "Don't bloody break that!"

"That's what I told him, boss!" Johannes had appeared, leaning over the edge of the boat "It's the base of the sluicing mechanism. That breaks, machine's done. Pack up and go home."

Doug manoeuvred the precious piece of material under my shattered leg, strapping me firmly to it with a length of para cord.

"How's that?"

"Terrible."

"Good. Jeff and Colin are going to lift your body, I'm going to get the legs. Ready? One, two –"

They lifted on two and I bit down hard on my jaw in anticipation of the pain but either Doug knew his business or the fentanyl had dulled my senses further than I thought because the expected pain did not materialise.

As they awkwardly clambered over the side of the boat I stared around. The spotlights had been trained towards the land and I saw that were on a narrow strip of shoreline, rocky at the beach where we stood but swiftly giving way to hefty pine trees that spread up through a small crevice that looked like a pass out of the canyon. I made to point this out but Doug stumbled as he stepped over the side and my leg moved, prompting such agony that there was no space for more thoughts in my head.

They laid me down in what was already looking like a camp. The efficiency of Solly and his troops was impressive and already several tents were up in a tight ring and Martin was laying a taut guide wire around the perimeter. Doug got me inside the larger of the tents we'd brought, designed to house the X Flare components and any other stores we couldn't leave outdoors. It wasn't a great solution but we planned on constructing a crude cabin to replace it. For now, I was laid down and Doug chased everyone but Solly from the tent.

"How bad is it?" Solly wanted to know.

"Bad." Doug was examining my shin "Do you know what happened?"

I shook my head but Solly had seen,

"After you went in, I grabbed the wheel and pointed us back downstream. Gibbo went past you with the current so I pulled him back on board but that made the boat swing towards the rock and your leg went between them."

I nodded slowly as though he'd made a profound point. The fentanyl was making me want to giggle "So it's your fault?"

Solly shot a finger at me before turning back to Doug "Do we need to evacuate?"

"No!" I gasped "We're bloody here now."

Doug ignored me "I can't make a full assessment without an x-ray but it might need surgery."

"Or you could just set it." I argued.

"Can he travel?" Solly asked.

Doug shrugged "Maybe. The pain will be bad though."

"More fentanyl." I agreed, nodding.

"What about the trees?" Solly asked, pointedly ignoring my babbling "Looked like they led to higher ground. If we could get him up there, we could get a helo."

Doug thought about it "Looked steep though."

"Fen-ta-nyl." I drew the word out and the two SAS soldiers looked at me as though I were a crackhead. I pressed my lips together.

"Can't do anything in the dark." Solly reasoned "Liam? We'll make a decision in the morning. By the way, Doug was a medic before he joined the Regiment and he was a paramedic before the army so you're in the best hands."

Doug held up both hands to illustrate the point comedically before beginning a series of checks of my vital signs and strapping my leg firmly to the sluice bed.

The drug began to lure me to sleep and I welcomed it, the fading adrenaline naturally adding to the drowsiness. As my thoughts began to lose focus, a sharp memory permeated them, a snatch of something I'd seen as the Nahanni greeted me with its icy embrace.

Gold flakes, floating like dust on a sunbeam.

Gold

CHAPTER 12

The next morning, I felt sick and my leg hurt. Doug brought me food and I pestered him into carrying me outside, propping me up against my kitbag as I stared around our camp. Fifty metres away, the river rushed wide and fast, turning a natural bend on the inside of which was the beach and strip of land that had given us our shelter. The entire thing was perhaps three hundred metres in depth, running from the cave filled walls of the canyon to the smooth shallows of the water. Further upstream, the land narrowed and even from my vantage point I could see it eventually faded out as the river straightened and the sheer walls of the canyon once again took over their towering majesty. Trees, thick evergreens sprawled across the ground like an infestation, the nearest only a dozen or so metres away. Already, Solly's men had marked a couple with white tape that I knew were candidates for felling, the wood would provide us with a heat source and the timber for a more permanent structure.

Expecting the ire of the rest of the expedition I braced myself for criticisms and filthy looks but to my surprise, everyone gathered around to check I was alright, genuine concern in their eyes with the exception of Gibbo who was helping Johannes with the X Flare down in the shallows.

"Brew?" Martin asked and I nodded eagerly, accepting a mug of earl grey with a powdered milk sachet in a china mug that read 'FYB'.

"Thanks." I muttered.

"How's it?" he sipped freeze dried coffee, wincing at the

terrible flavour as he crouched next to me, indicating my leg.

"I've had worse." I lied.

"Solly wants to send you back to Fort Simpson."

"Sod that!" I protested, spilling a drop of tea on my hand "Dose me up and splint it. No point going back now we're here."

"Might give you permanent injuries."

"The amount of gold I plan to scrape out of this place, I can buy myself a new leg." I knew I was being nonchalant. In truth, I was terrified that I'd done irreparable damage to the leg but the thought of enduring a painstaking journey back down the length of the Nahanni was unimaginable. Every bump or rapid would be like torture and I knew I'd rather sit here and sip tea.

"I don't think that was your fault with the boat." Martin hesitated, lowering his voice "I saw Gibbo wallowing about like a hippo at the front. There's no way you could have seen those rocks."

He was probably just trying to make me feel better but his words cheered me up immensely. I nodded gently to myself as I watched Gibbo and Johannes argue in the shallows over the X Flare.

"Match made in hell there." Martin followed my line of sight. He looked back to me "Anything you need?"

"Piss." I said and he laughed, promising to bring me a bottle "Keep an air hole at the top though when you go." he warned me.

"What? Like cut a hole?"

"No. When you shove your little todger in, make sure you leave a gap besides it. Shouldn't be too hard for you."

"Why?" I asked, bemused by the suggestion "What happens if I don't?"

Martin began to answer then smiled and laughed "Tell you what, try it without the air hole. Might be we need a laugh." he strolled off to find a bottle as Solly approached.

"I'm not going anywhere and you can't make me." I greeted him, provoking a smile.

"No. I think it's better if you stay here and Doug treats you."

Relief washed over me like a child being given permission by a parent. That annoyed me that Solly had assumed command over me in such a way and I merely grunted in response.

"He's just making you a proper splint." Solly glanced back over to the treeline which now the gloomy daylight had fully reached us I could see was thick with undergrowth.

"Better get this back to Johannes then." I indicated the makeshift splint we'd used yesterday and Solly helped me remove it, calling the South African back from the river.

Johannes was twitching more than usual with excitement at the prospect of the yellow metal "Don't suppose you saw any when you were down there last night, eh boss?" he joked as he brushed imaginary specks of dust from the sluice bed.

"Sparkly and glimmering." I grinned, remembering the hallucination.

"Ooh. You should be a writer using words like that." Was his parting shot as he hurried back to the shore to fit the piece of carbon.

Doug returned with an armful of freshly cut wood which stank of sap.

"Need to do a bit more examining." he explained and lifted the jacket I'd covered my leg with. He then proceeded to prod and squeeze the broken bone with far more force than was necessary, earning him a colourful critique of his personality, ancestry, and the general population of Scotland.

"I'm actually not pro-independence." he observed mildly as activity paused in the camp to eavesdrop. I could see broad smiles on almost every face and extended my insults to the rest of them, provoking laughter which brought Johannes' head up from the X Flare like a startled horse.

"Alright." Doug sat back on his haunches "It's actually pretty clean. The two ends of the bone are a bit disjointed though." He placed a careful finger and I looked, seeing a small lump.

"Doesn't look too bad?" I observed.

"No. But we'll have to set it."

I began to ask but Doug just smiled and handed me a thick wad of bitter tasting tree bark. I glowered at him as I held it between my teeth.

The independence loving, tam o'shanter wearing, whisky for blood having, bog peat dwelling pixie poxed puffbag punched my leg bones back into place.

"Is that whisky with an 'e' or not?" he asked as I howled.

"Your Mum's got an 'e'!" I roared as Solly cracked up beside me. I spat pine bark out of my mouth.

"It's pronounced 'Mam'." Doug corrected.

I turned my head to the side and vomited up the cup of tea that Martin had brought me before collapsing backwards onto my bag "Is that what they teach you in the SAS?" I demanded.

"Nah. I learned that in Glasgow." Doug retorted.

"Buggering Scotch tosspot." I grated and he grinned, setting to splinting my leg.

Having failed to torture me to death, he now fashioned what he called a survival splint involving two lengths of pine, one long and one short. The longer length went on the outside of my leg, coming up as high as my armpit where I wrapped several layers of spare clothing around it to protect myself from the jagged wood. The shorter end was strapped to the inside of the leg, the two protruding several inches below my foot. Doug then fashioned a cross member that joined the two sturdy pieces, wrapping several layers of duct tape around to hold it in place.

"Can I walk on that?" I looked at it sceptically and Doug shook his head.

"You aren't going anywhere for at least a couple of days. After that, I'll make you some crutches and you can hobble around camp at least.

I rolled my eyes "Bring me some wood. I'll start now. It'll probably take me two days at least."

Doug couldn't argue with that and moved off as I tried and failed to wrap my trouser leg around the wood.

"Bloody thing." I swore, the cold air already biting at my skin. Solly helped me pull on my boots which, with the help of a pair of Gore-Tex socks would dry out from the soaking they'd got yesterday. That still left my leg bare though and so I took the still damp pair of trousers that Doug had sliced yesterday and began to cut them further, tying them in strips around the makeshift splint so that in the end I looked like a homeless man, down on his luck.

"Fetching." Martin had come over with a fresh mug of tea to replace the one I'd vomited.

I affected a wounded air as I sipped it.

"This is for you." he dumped a hefty looking rifle next to me along with a set of body armour.

I cocked an eyebrow.

"See, out here there's plenty of nasties that want to gobble you up. Bears, wolves and nasty head-chomping ghoulies." He leered at me "And right now, you're like meals not-on-wheels."

"Very droll."

"I try. Anyway, keep these handy, will you?"

I pulled the body armour on, appreciating the extra layer of warmth it provided and noting the spare magazines stuffed into the pouches at the front.

"Martin." I called as he turned away "Are you here to fight a war or something?"

He gave me a quizzical look and hurried away. I frowned, wondering not for the first time if there was something I was missing. I couldn't fathom Solly's real reason for this cache of weapons he'd brought. At least, not with the hundreds of rounds of ammunition he'd lugged along. Earlier, the idea of blatting a few thousand bullets into the treeline had seemed like a good idea but now that we were here, the towering canyon walls looked oppressive and I couldn't see anyone emptying a magazine without the noise blasting all our eardrums to shreds. Still...

"GOLD!" Johannes' voice erupted like a volcano from the riverbank. Echoing off the cave filled rock faces and drawing every eye to him he stood with both hands over his head, grinning from ear to ear, his eyes wide and burning with what I could now see clearly for the first time that which Adam had called Gold Fever.

CHAPTER 13

Gold! More specifically, gold dust. And not just a few flecks of it! The Chinese had built their machine well and Johannes was able to carry a cupful of the shining yellow powder to wave under my nose.

"Gold! Good gold, too! I knew it, boss! I bloody knew it!"

"Gold!" I shouted, my voice filling the canyon and the SAS soldiers came bounding back over, delight and reverence on every face. We'd done it!

A babble of voices rose, drowning out the sound of the river for the first time since we'd arrived. The cup was passed from hand to hand, every man prodding or poking the glimmering treasure like a curious schoolboy.

"How much?" someone asked and Johannes, face locked into a gleaming grin began a long winded explanation of weights and expected yields which I half listened to, staring in amazement at the mug with its bounty. I realised that a part of me had doubted we'd find anything and the crash followed by my injury had lowered my expectations to the point where simply stubbornly searching for a few weeks would have satisfied me that it wasn't a wasted trip.

"Can we get more?" Gibbo wasn't smiling but the same excitement filled his voice as every other man there.

"River gives what it wants." Niimi suddenly spoke up with his trademark dour expression and I started, fully having forgotten our two native guides were still with us.

"Well, it bloody wants to give us gold!" Johannes barked, his disdain for the two men not forgotten but pride suffusing his tones in the joy at the discovery. Abruptly, he snatched the cup back and stalked back down to the X Flare, Gibbo going with him and immediately began the sifting process again.

"Success!" I grinned at Solly who stood close by. He shot me a small smile then turned to look at the treeline a few metres away.

"I'm going to take a look up that hill." he announced, indicating the narrow and treacherously steep strip of hillside that provided an unexpected exit from the valley.

I stared after him as he pressed Jeff and Andy into following him, the three moving off in an standard patrol formation.

"What was that all about?" I asked Doug as he bent to check on my splint.

He shrugged and looked uncomfortable "Solly reckons there's something 'off' about this place."

I snorted "Of course there is. It's called 'Headless Valley', remember?"

Doug snorted in response but there was little humour in it.

"Oh, come on." I scoffed "Look, there are enough real dangers out here without making up some superstitious nonsense, aren't there?" I indicated my ruined leg as an example.

"Aye." Doug looked embarassed "It's not that I believe or disbelieve any stories – I prefer on evidence, you know? Give me some proof theres a monster that has a taste for human heads and I'll believe it but until then, jury's out."

"Right." I agreed, nodding as his thoughts echoed my own.

"But Solly doesn't get a 'feeling' without merit." Doug stared after the small patrol that had now vanished into the treeline "If he reckons there's something wrong, there could well be."

"Alright, I'll buy that his instincts are good." I allowed "But all we're talking about there is his biology. Like, we're programmed to detect danger, aren't we? As humans I mean. It's an evolutionary thing. That's where all these stories come from. People have come here looking for gold or for whatever and a lot of them have died. It makes sense we'd build stories around that and embellish them as a warning to ourselves."

"Aye, I'm not claiming he's psychic or anything!" Doug chuckled "But like you say, the instinct is there for a reason and it's based on something your subconscious has noticed, isn't it?"

I allowed that it probably was.

"So I reckon his subconscious has seen something that's set him off."

"Yeah, a hundred feet of sheer rock in every direction, me with a broken leg and the nearest human habitation a week away. Everyone is going to be twitchy."

Doug raised an eyebrow "Quite the sceptic, aren't you?"

I shrugged "I'm as sceptical as anyone else. Like you said, show me some evidence and then I'll agree. Otherwise, it's not about belief. Belief isn't real, evidence is."

Doug thought about that for a moment.

I continued "There's plenty of danger around here. I can't say it's a bad thing that Solly has got an itchy trigger finger. Who knows, maybe he finds a pack of grizzlies in the woods and takes them all out before they get us?" I looked hopefully towards the wood line as though I expected shots to ring out "But wildlife and hypothermia are bad enough without made up stories."

I thought I might have impressed Doug with my reasoning or maybe he'd decided this wasn't the place for an intellectual debate. In any case, the sour faced Scot finished his checks in a thoughtful silence. Niimi, the closest of our two native guests had wandered over, clearly eavesdropping on the conversation.

"Alright there, pal?" Doug watched him warily.

"Sorry to listen." Niimi spoke in staccato sentences. It was a little odd to hear "Heard you talk about the valley."

"Oh?" I cocked an eyebrow "What about the legends then?"

"Not just legends." he sat down next to us as comfortable on the hard ground as any Englishman on a sofa "You know how the river got it's name?"

"From the Naha tribe." I recalled from my research "They vanished."

"Naha kept these lands." Niimi lifted his hands to illustrate the valley surrounding us "Kept the balance, made their offerings."

"What offerings?"

"Tobacco, food, even men sometimes."

"A good old human sacrifice, eh?" Doug joked but I saw the concern in his face.

Niimi regarded him coolly "Ritual keeps the balance. We give the offering, the valley lets us pass. More people come here now. More times we need to do the ritual."

Doug rolled his eyes "That's what you're here for?"

Niimi nodded seriously "We walk the Naha's lands now. We keep the balance."

I felt a shiver run down my spine "So, what do you offer the valley?" I asked.

"Food. Tobacco." He drew an ornamental, carved wooden handled knife from his belt "Things like this."

"Not men?"

"No. Valley don't want men now." He returned the knife to its sheath.

Disappointment flooded through me. The creepy voice had had me going for a moment but now Niimi just sounded ridiculous. I wondered when his group had started performing the ritual, whether it was before or after the tourists started flooding in. Somehow it was hard to parse the idea of canoeists with their bright waterproofs and gas fired camping stoves being worried by the legends of the Headless Valley. I shook my head as Niimi, his creepy warning delivered trudged back to his tent.

Doug rolled his eyes at me and we both shared a grin. As he stood to leave and take his turn with Johannes on the X Flare, he lowered his head and muttered to me quietly enough that Niimi wouldn't hear "All this superstitious stuff, at least we made that tobacco offering to the river, eh?"

That made us both roar with derisive laughter as he headed down to the Gold.

Solly returned with Jeff and Andy at the slow, trudging pace of a soldier on patrol. He reported they'd climbed most of the way up the steep slope but were stopped at the top by an almost sheer rock face. They could probably have climbed it, Solly explained but saw no need to take the risk without the ropes and harnesses we'd brought on the boats. I felt a small surge of pride that I'd thought to purchase those as we'd arrived in Canada. Johannes had scoffed as I haggled over the price, insisting that if anything, we needed scuba gear to access the bounty of the Nahanni but I'd had a nagging worry in my head about the unmapped caves that were now in plain sight and thought in an emergency we might need to scramble into one of them for shelter.

The daylight was already failing as Doug brought me a sturdy collection of pine branches that I set about whittling into a pair of crutches, glad to have a project. Johannes had finally abandoned the gold sifting, allowing that there was no rush and sitting down with his notebook to record in painstaking detail exactly when and how he'd sifted the gold.

"Good day today, gents." Solly nodded around the camp as we ate an evening meal from boiled ration packs.

There were murmurs of assent, the loudest from Johannes who had stopped grinning – probably to rest his facial muscles – but was still as exuberant as ever, chewing the ears off anyone foolish enough to sit close.

"Tomorrow I'm going up that cliff and seeing whats at the top." Solly announced "Doug, I want you with me in case anyone has a drama with the climbing.

Doug hesitated before answering "Seems a bit of a risk, mate. I know you want to get a feel for the land but these rocks aren't that stable. Be an awful shame if we got another casualty.

Solly nodded as though he'd expected the question and flicked a glance at me "Liam? What do you think?"

I was surprised to be asked but pleased he was involving me "I – look, we all came here to take risks, didn't we?"

That elicited some shrugs from the group.

"The thing I'm thinking, Solly, is what's got your back up so badly?"

I hadn't phrased the question well and I felt the bristling

from the men gathered around the small campfire we'd started. People didn't talk to Solly in that way. Not in front of his blokes, anyway.

"No –" Solly held up a hand "It's a fair question." He met the eyes of the SAS guys "You all know why we're here. Frankly, I'm not much use on the X Flare and our Afrikaner friend here seems to have it all under control."

"Yup." Johannes' voice was dripping with satisfaction. He grinned at anyone who met his eye.

"I reckon my job here is to keep the camp safe, particularly now Liam is man-down." he indicated my leg "To that end, I want to know what's around us."

I wanted to say more, about how the stories were superstitious nonsense but I didn't want to draw the ire of the rest of the group by making Solly look foolish. Instead, I nodded. If Solly wanted to go rock climbing, it was his business.

"Alright." a silent agreement had been reached "Jeff? You're the best climber." the grey haired soldier nodded.

"And I'll come fix you when you forget to tie the rope off." Doug interjected to shouts of laughter and a glower from Solly at some in-joke in which clearly Solly was the butt.

"Are we keeping a sentry?" I asked, a question that on any training exercise would have roused the fury of the other soldiers who'd be silently praying the chain of command had forgotten to post a roster and we'd be given a night of undisturbed sleep. Out here the thought of someone or something wandering into our camp was very real and I'd fancy my chances a whole lot better with an armed guard.

There were general murmurs of agreement and Martin volunteered to write out a roster giving us all an hour during the night. I tried to be placed on it, insisting I had my rifle and after sitting around all day on my arse I hardly needed the same amount of sleep but he ignored me. As it was, the painful and laborious process of getting into my sleeping bag took almost an hour and when I finally squeezed into my tent, Johannes immediately knocked the injured limb causing me to attempt a new world record in combinations of curses and I volunteered to spend the night back where I'd spent the day, under the stars.

With a great deal of sweat and curses I found a space to spread a roll mat, keeping the worst of the cold ground away from my body and pulled the waterproof bivvy over my head, sleep taking me almost at once.

I woke in the night with a desperately full bladder and did my usual trick with the bottle, hoping in the darkness I'd left the required airhole and avoided the clever urine spraying trick Doug had warned me of. I sighed with relief as the pressure in my abdomen faded and I heard a chuckle in the darkness next to me, recognising Jeff's voice.

"Pissing the bed, STAB?" he asked.

"Come closer and find out." I dared him and he sniggered.

"Why am I out here again?" he asked me.

"Gold, riches and fame." I reminded him, zipping my doss bag back up against the chill night air "But if you don't want it you can leave us your share and foxtrot-oscar..."

"Oh yeah. You'd love that, wouldn't you?" he jabbed me in the ribs and I swatted back but missed in the darkness.

"Careful, STAB! You know I've got three black belts and you've got a gammy leg!"

"Why don't you tie them all into a noose and –"

The shriek of a whistle cut the air and we froze into silence.

My heart pumping in my ears was the only sound until:

Peeeee-hoooo

"What the bloody shit was that?" Jeff hissed.

For some reason, the nervousness in his voice frightened me more than whatever night creature was making the sound. He, an SAS veteran who was as tough as old boots sounded *scared*.

"A bird." I said but even to me my voice sounded unsure. I'd shoved the rifle between my sleeping bag and bivvy as was the standard in the army but I drew it out, suddenly feeling vulnerable on my back.

There was a clicking sound as Jeff fished a pair of night vision binoculars from a pouch and began to scan the camp methodically. My eyes had adjusted a little to the darkness and I could make out his shape kneeling next to me, turning at intervals to survey other areas.

Peeeee-hoooo

The sound was closer now and both our heads snapped in the direction of the river where the X Flare still sat in the shallows.

"It's moving..." Jeff was staring through the binoculars at the river.

"Can you see it?"

"No..."

Peeeee-hoooo

Now it was behind us and I twisted uselessly, hampered by my leg and improvised cast.

"Anything?"

"No. Shut up."

"What's going on?" Solly's voice was low and calm and then he was there, a dark shadow melting out of the gloom to kneel beside me.

"Noise." Jeff reported.

"Here." Solly took the binos, staring around the camp.

Peeeee-hoooo

Solly wasn't given to exclamations but the silence and stillness that came from him was reaction enough. I felt sweat form on my palms,

Peeeee-hoooo

"There!" Solly turned to the nearest tent, the one I'd vacated just a couple of hours before and where Johannes now lay.

"Sod this –" Jeff suddenly stood and a tearing sound followed by the whoosh of a rocket and glaring light erupted over the camp as he shot a flare, suspended by a parachute into the night sky.

"Stand-to!" roared Solly and there was a general, sleep muffled echo of the order as men rolled out of sleeping bags and fought tent zippers. I heard more than one rifle being cocked and a shout for instructions.

Peeeee-hoooo

Peeeee-hoooo

Peeeee-hoooo

Three more of the high pitched whistles in quick succession, all from the same place.

"Treeline!" shouted someone and I held my breath, waiting for the onslaught of gunfire that would tear pine needles from the boughs.

"Target indication?" called a voice I recognised as Gibbo's.

There was silence.

Peeeee-hoooo

Moving away now but definitely towards the treeline.

"A bird?" someone suggested again.

"Shut it!" Solly snarled, his cool finally broken. Next to him, Jeff shot another flare into the sky as the first began to fall to earth.

A rustling of canvas and a thick stream of curses and Johannes' head emerged from his tent, his hair pointing in all different directions and still in his sleeping bag.

"What about the machine?" he demanded and when no-one answered he frantically tore open his sleeping bag and ran through the camp down to the shoreline.

"Get back here!" a handful of voices roared but Johannes was gone, past the ring of the flare light. Jeff shot a third flare up, cursing the South African.

"It's alright!" his clipped tones reached us clearly "Machine is fine. Gold's still here. Someone help me move it!"

The whistling was gone. Johannes was apparently unaware or uncaring of the fact we were being stalked in the darkness and we could all hear the grunting sounds he made as he began to haul the first box of the gold back over the rough ground towards the camp.

"Should've kept it here anyway!" he swore as Solly moved over to shut the man up.

"There's something out there!" he hissed at the Gold-mad African.

"What? That whistling? Just a bird! Stop your flapping!" he

snarled and I felt the hesitation around the camp. Had it just been a night bird? The third flare burned out and Jeff didn't fire another one. Voices called questions which Solly didn't have the answers to.

"Stand down!" Jeff called suddenly "Dunno what that was. Everyone keep your weapons handy! Could be local wildlife."

There was silence. I thought about asking the two locals but in the darkness, I couldn't tell where they were and I was feeling foolish about the alarm we'd caused.

There was no more weird whistling that night. At some point, I managed to fall asleep although I'd sworn to myself I'd stay awake all night. The grey dawn over the top of the rock faces brought me awake and I turned my head to see that Andy was now on sentry next to me, his gaze watchful.

"Anything more?" I asked quietly and he shook his head as around us the camp began to stir.

Johannes moved before the others, heading back down to the shoreline once again to confirm the X Flare was still there which it was. He examined the gold he'd gathered yesterday, confident that none had vanished overnight to our mysterious visitor. As he trudged back to camp for breakfast, he stopped and I caught a glimpse of him ducking and staring into the open tent that our two native guests had shared.

A stream of Afrikaans curses filled the air and once again, we were on alert because the natives were gone.

CHAPTER 14

"At least we know what the noises were." Jeff opined as Martin began to collapse the now vacant tent.

"Do we?" I asked, "How did they make that whistle?"

He frowned and began to concentrate his lips and fingers into ever more complicated patterns, trying in vain to recreate the eerie sound.

"Anyway –" I continued "If they were sneaking off then why would they make those noises? It nearly got them shot."

"I bloody said we shouldn't have brought them!" Johannes raged "Can't trust the red-skinned bastards! They saw the gold and now look!"

"The locals aren't thieves." Gibbo argued "They're just hunters. They've got no interest at all in Gold dust."

"Then why'd they leave the night we found some, huh?" Johannes rounded on Gibbo, ignoring the fact that Gibbo outweighed him by half as much again.

"Probably had enough of your little racist mouth." Gibbo snarled and Martin had to step between them to stop punches being thrown.

"Either way, this settles things." Solly spoke over the tension "I'll take Doug and Jeff back up the hill. Martin? You go as far up the riverbank as you can get following the shoreline then come back through the trees." he pointed and every face leaned out to look down the length of our spit of land.

No time was wasted. I of course stayed sat where I was, whittling the crutches to take my mind off the whistling sound and the missing natives whilst Johannes got the gold sluicing back underway. Solly left with Jeff and Doug and all our climbing equipment, vanishing into the trees. Martin took Gibbo, pointedly keeping him away from Johannes, and Robbie went with them, heading down the shoreline.

Boredom set in quickly. I'd whittled the crutches down to a passable set and I spent a few moments trying to stand, finding that my balance was appalling after two days sat on the floor and agony racked me as the broken bones moved. Still, there was nothing else to do and last night had been a wonderful motivator to get me moving and by the time noon rolled around, I was on my feet. Well, *foot,* specifically. The crutches were alright although one creaked alarmingly as I shuffled a couple of paces.

"Steady on!" called Andy from the shoreline. He and Colin were the only two SAS men left and so far they were the two I knew the least. I waved to show them I was alright and in the process, dropped my rifle. Andy hurried over.

"Sorry." I muttered as he slung the weapon back over my shoulder.

"Not much use to you when you're on those, is it?" he observed, sceptically "You'd fall over if you fired it. Here..."

He led me over to the large tent we were using as storage and held open the flap for me. Inside were the stacks of crates that Solly had insisted we bring. Andy pulled a black rugged crate the size of an ordinary briefcase and laid it atop a stack, popping the clasp.

"Here." Inside was a hefty looking pistol of a type I didn't recognise. With it was a holster which would attach to my belt. Andy began pulling out spare magazines "Stuff these in your pocket and keep this on your hip. It's a .45 so a bit bigger than the Glock you'll be used to. It won't stop a grizzly but it'll certainly put it off. Much better that trying to fumble that rifle." he added.

Grateful, I thanked him although I felt foolish with the bulky handgun on my hip like something out of a bad western. I set my sights on the treeline as Andy headed back to shore and began the long and grim process of crossing the rough ground.

Over an hour later and I discovered that squatting with a broken leg was impossible. That made the very overdue task of relieving myself that was the sole reason I'd come this way a major challenge and the clenching of my stomach and foul aroma I was emitting in noisy bursts gave me a sense of urgency that forced me to settle for resting on a sticky bough which bent alarmingly under my weight as I let out a long sigh of relief.

The necessary covering with pine needles and redressing myself took another interminable length of time and I'd been gone long enough for Andy and Colin to shoot ribald comments at me as I slowly limped back to the camp. I made my way down to the shoreline to where the three of them were working the X Flare, awkwardly leaning on the stern of the closest boat to wash my hands in the river.

"Phwoar!" Andy pinched his nose in mock disgust "Did you step in your own mess, STAB?"

I shot him the finger and he pretended to inspect the nail for dirt, shaking his head in mock disgust.

"Any word from Solly?" I asked when the necessary ritual of banter was complete and he shook his head, tapping the handheld radio on his belt.

"Useless down here. No signal with all these rocks." He pointed at the canyon walls.

"Won't he get signal up the top?" I stared up to the top of the cave studded sides where bright sunlight was visible, far out of reach.

"Might do." Andy nodded We'd all seen the caves and his words seemed to echo our thoughts "Reckon those caves lead anywhere?"

"Must do." I agreed "Why?"

"See – " Andy leaned back to stretch his lower back from where he'd been bent over the machine "I did a bit of reading myself before coming out here. Those two brothers that lost their heads…"

"The McLeod brothers."

"Yeah. They panned for gold but then they found a mine." he

gestured around "Can't see anywhere they'd have done that but inside the caves."

I was sceptical "If the gold was near the river then surely they dug around here?"

"Nah." Andy was emphatic "Dig too close to the water and you'll just get a wet hole. Has to be back from the edge a little." He gestured at the closest rock face "Even *you* could get into those caves." indeed, the lowest of the yawning mouths was barely six feet above the ground although the entrance was no more than half my height.

"Why don't you go looking then?" I joked "We could use one less person to share all this with." I pointed at the X Flare.

"Maybe I will! And when I come back with a nugget, you can all suck a –"

"No! No, no, no!" Johannes frantic voice suddenly filled the air and we whipped around to where he and Colin were both staring in horror at the complex looking machine as the carbon bottom of the sluice tray, the same part Doug had fashioned as a splint for my leg, suddenly dropped into the flow of the river.

Johannes dived after it, sending a spray of water as the thin black object was swept further out into the current.

"Get back here you bloody idiot!" Andy snarled but Johannes ignored him, now up to his waist in the fast flowing Nahanni.

"Get the boat!" I shouted and turned to sit on the edge of the closest Raider. I half fell in, miraculously managing not to injure my leg further and frantically levered myself around to sit in the pilot's chair.

"Colin!" Andy shouted and the second man turned, joining Andy at the bows and together they shoved the craft out into the stream as I whipped the engine into life.

The current took us and I urged the boat closer to shore where the stream was gentlest, heedless of the grating sound we made in the shallow draught. Colin was looping a rope around his waist, tying a frantic knot whilst Andy lashed the far end to a metal ring mounted on the hull for that exact purpose.

"Got it!" we heard a shout as I levered the craft to face towards

Johannes and we were just in time to see the South African grip the piece of carbon in both hands and vanish beneath the surface, bobbing back up a second later.

I thrust the throttle open and we leapt forwards, almost immediately pulling the control back and shoving the motor into reverse thrust as we came alongside the stricken man who was spluttering, utterly unable to use his arms to keep afloat.

A splash, and Colin was overboard, grabbing Johannes and shouting at him to let the piece go but Johannes stubbornly clung on and now Andy was trying to pull them both aboard as the boat tilted alarmingly and the current hauled us out into the centre.

"Get the bloody part!" I snarled at Andy and he abandoned trying to shout at Johannes, instead seizing the vital piece of carbon and flinging it unceremoniously into the bottom of the hull before tugging the drenched African aboard. I steered hard to compensate as river water spilled over the sides, pooling in the bottom of the Raider but then Johannes was gasping and choking and Colin was being pulled out with Andy's help and I shoved the throttle open, turning regain control and bringing us in a wide, gentle loop back towards our landing ground.

I ran us ashore, killing the engine and we all stayed still, utterly soaked and panting.

"Bloody machine won't work without it." Johannes spat from the pool of river water that now weighed us down.

"Wasn't worth drowning for." Colin muttered.

Johannes' silent disagreement was palpable as he panted to recover. Andy and Colin helped me out of the boat, retrieving one of my crutches which dropped into the water. Johannes climbed out himself, his long hair plastered to his skull and giving him an even more crazed look. He quickly examined the carbon part, moving back to the X Flare which Andy and Colin then had to help lever out of the shallows for him to examine it.

"Just screw it back on?" I asked hopefully but Andy who had squatted down to stare at the underside of the mechanism was shaking his head and pointing something out to Johannes.

"Agh!" the Afrikaner pounded a fist on the small stones of the beach "We should never have used this for a splint – I told that bloody Scotsman! Agh!"

"The mechanism kept running when the bottom fell off." Andy explained, standing up with a rueful look on his face "It's burned through the brushes that separate the Gold from the sediment. The carbon base must have been part of the cooling process."

"We can fix it!" Johannes had produced a neatly packaged screwdriver set and was already carefully dismantling the X Flare.

Andy looked sceptical but Johannes was pointing at some complicated component that was beyond my understanding.

"That's not going to hold-"

"It is! We just need –"

"I think –"

"Hmm…"

I limped over to the camp as the two of them pored over the details, peering at the treeline in hopes of seeing Martin's patrol returning but only the forbidding barrier of the trees and the constant rushing of the river greeted my gaze.

I began to fret as the lack of returning soldiers and the frantic actions of Andy and Johannes worked my stress levels up a few degrees. Colin, having changed out of his wet clothes and laid them out to dry came and joined me.

"Bloody mess this is turning out to be."

"It could be going better." I agreed.

"No word from Solly." he wiggled the small radio in his hand.

"Or Martin?" I pointed down the strip of land "He should be back by now."

"Maybe they found something." Colin shrugged. He turned to look at the steep slope where Solly had headed and together we worked out the rock face that had caused the patrol to take the climbing equipment with them. Muttering, Colin vanished into his tent returning a few moments later with an expensive pair or binoculars that he trained on the rockface.

"Well?" I prompted when he stood silent for almost a full minute.

In response, he handed me the binos and I trained them, adjusting the lenses a little and twiddling the focus dial until the silvery rock came into view.

"Can you see the ropes?" Colin asked and I frowned, locking onto the thin black cord that flapped in the faint breeze.

"Looks like they've already gone up."

"Yeah. Except the rope is only anchored halfway up."

I stared, frowning until I saw that the black climbing rope was indeed only anchored midway up the almost sheer rock face. There were no climbers in sight and it wasn't high enough to allow Solly or the others to reach the top and vanish from sight.

"Weird."

"Yeah. Do you know anything about climbing?"

I shook my head. The last time I'd climbed had been an indoor wall at the HAC and I'd got about four metres up before my arms gave out and I now avoided the activity like the plague.

"We all do a bit in the Regiment." Colin explained "But if they got high enough to make that anchor point and didn't go any further that means they went back down. Why would they go back down?"

"Maybe the rock wasn't safe enough?" I suggested.

"Surely they'd have taken the anchor point out on the way back down?" Colin sounded doubtful. He tried the radio, turning the volume up so I could hear the static that filled the airwaves. He called Solly, then Martin but got no response, repeating the summons a few times before returning the device to his belt.

"The thing I'm worried about is maybe someone fell." Colin dared to state what we'd both been thinking.

"But the anchor point?"

"Yeah…"

We were spared further speculation by the arrival of a grim looking Andy and Johannes.

"A week." Johannes spat out.

"To fix it?"

Andy nodded "We need to take the whole thing apart. I think we can do it but it'll take time."

"A week seems awfully specific." I wasn't trying to sound suspicious.

"Maybe it'll be quicker." Johannes shrugged "We've got to get it right though, boss. No point us being here otherwise."

"And we haven't got enough Gold to go back yet." I pointed at the scant pile we'd retrieved thus far.

Johannes shrugged at the obviousness of the statement "Nothing else for it. We'll bring the machine inside the storage tent. Got to move the other stuff out first though."

Unable to help, I was given the binoculars and the radio and told to stand on watch whilst the other three sweated and grunted, stacking the various crates and boxes out in the open and lashing a basha over the top to protect from the elements. I half watched the crates, wondering why Solly had brought so much in our three small boats. Then again, his absence was like a constant throbbing as I stared intently at the now flapping rope that hung from the cliff face.

"Hey!" Andy had paused to stretch his back again and was now pointing. I followed his line of sight to the shoreline where Martin, followed by Gibbo and Robbie was trudging back towards camp.

"Where've you been?" Colin and Andy greeted him as Gibbo eyed the stack of crates suspiciously.

"Woods were too thick." Martin explained, curious about the crates "We ended up going back to the riverbank then moving along to get back into the woods each time. Took a little while." He held up his radio "No signal?"

"None." I filled him in on the details and dramas of the day, explaining the damage to the X Flare which brought a round of swearing from Gibbo although they all went quiet when we told them of Solly's absence and each took their turn looking up at the cliff face.

"Why'd they leave the anchor?" Robbie broke the confused silence.

No-one answered as Martin took the binos back and stared "That rope isn't anchored at the base." He suddenly pointed out.

"What?"

Gibbo had a second pair of binos and he stared up, cursing as he spotted whatever Martin was seeing. I grabbed Martin's pair and stared, seeing what he meant.

Where the rope led up to the anchor in the rockface it was taut and clearly well secured at the base of the cliff, out of our line of sight because of the trees. But the second line that we could make out, the part that I'd expect to be attached to the climber was dangling freely, occasionally flapping in the wind.

"It's been cut!" I exclaimed.

"But it must have reached the top." Gibbo was reasoning slowly "They must have gone up the rock face and then it broke away from whatever they anchored it to up there. That's why its loose."

It was no small measure of relief to realise that there was no shattered body lying at the foot of the cliff. Gibbo's explanation made sense and as the binos were passed around again, there were murmurs of agreement.

"They might not have noticed." Andy pointed out "If they climbed over the top and moved off, they won't find out its cut until they get back."

"Do they have enough rope to make another anchor?" I asked.

No-one could say. Without knowing exactly how much they'd used to scale the cliff and with the strong possibility there was another rock face waiting over the top, we were stuck guessing. Martin seemed to take over in Solly's absence and he wasted little time in keeping us busy. I was given the binoculars and instructed not to take my eyes off the cliff face whilst Johannes, Andy and Gibbo began the long process of dismantling the X Flare.

"Over here." Martin directed the laborious restacking of all the kit we'd moved out of our large tent. I shot surreptitious glances at a few of the boxes, some of which were unmistakably weapons crates and wondered again how much firepower Solly had brought. The line of climbing rope flapped in the breeze as the wind picked up making a faint whistling sound.

"Was that what we heard last night?" I wondered out loud but Colin who was closest shook his head.

"Nah. It wasn't this windy then anyway."

I grunted in response. In any case, the sound of the gusts through the canyon was utterly different from the weird noises that had woken us last night and was unmistakable as any other sound.

Finally, the light was clearly beginning to fail and Martin had stopped working, staring up at the cliff face with a worried look. Even Johannes had emerged from the tent, looking warily from the forest to the tops of the canyons as Martin spoke into the radio, trying in vain to raise Solly.

"Should we go up there?" I asked Martin.

He shrugged "Not much chance of getting there now. It'll be dark in half an hour and those woods are thick.

The temperature was dropping.

"Did they have sleeping bags?"

"No."

"Have we got more climbing gear?"

"No."

"But surely the rope that's there – we can just send another climber up and secure it?"

"We don't have a harness…" Martin tailed off "We could do it, yeah. Alright."

He gathered us around, looking at the stressed faces "Today was a shit show, gents. Tomorrow will be better. We have to assume that Solly and the others have hit a snag but we can't get up that cliff face in the dark."

Colin started to protest but Martin held up a hand.

"I know you want to but if we get another casualty, we're starting to reduce our chances of ever getting out of here. Doug is our best medic, remember and without him we might well lose someone if they take a tumble off those rocks. We need to be sensible."

No-one argued.

"Two of us on stag tonight at all times. Everyone has a rifle and a full loadout of magazines. If you're sleeping in the tents, leave them unzipped and your boots on in case we need to bug out. Get the Gold on the boats and turn them so they're ready to launch in a hurry. Get some food on them, too."

The SAS soldiers scurried to make these arrangements, leaving me in the centre of the camp. I'd retrieved my rifle and now kept it slung across my body whilst I used the last of the light to stare in vain for our missing men.

Movement...

"Martin!" I snapped and he hurried over. The binos were still pressed to my eyes and he had the second pair "Above the rope, a little to the left. Do you –"

"Got him!" he shouted "Lads, get eyes on the cliff face, now!"

I didn't take the binos away from my eyes to see who was able to gather the necessary magnification but I heard a couple of curses that surely meant others saw what I saw.

"That's the one that didn't come with us, right?" Martin called.

"One hundred percent." Gibbo grunted a response, proving he'd found something to bring the top of the cliff into focus.

"Benji or something?"

"Bineshii." I murmured as the face of the native, silhouetted by the dying light at the top of the cliff gazed down at the suddenly terrified camp.

CHAPTER 15

We stared at Bineshii until the light blocked him from view. In all that time, perhaps a handful of minutes he didn't move, didn't even seem to blink although it was impossible to be sure from this distance. He was looking at us, that much was clear from the angle of his neck but he could have been a statue for all the life he showed.

Gibbo had sighted with a long range rifle although the man was well out of range and protected by the strong winds that now drove the severed rope to whip back and forth. Then darkness fell and we could no longer see him.

"First light, we're going up that cliff and I'm getting answers from that bloke." Martin promised and the soldiers settled in for the night. No-one slept much although we were spared the appalling whistling sound that had disturbed us the night before. Instead, my dreams were racked by the faces of Bill and Niimi, our ostensible guides who cackled as they flung handfuls of Gold dust in my face, taking it in turns to remove their laughing heads from their torsos, making me flinch awake and reach for the comforting weight of the rifle.

Martin was moving before dawn. He assembled four men, all of them dressed in full combat gear. Now wasn't the time for difficult questions and I admit I was even grateful to see the grenades, spare magazines and the bulk of a belt fed FN Minimi machine gun that Gibbo seemed to weigh in his hands with relish. Colin and Robbie made up the squad, Colin now clutching the scoped rifle that Gibbo had scooped up last night. They set off for the treeline before the light was strong enough to see them leave and vanished into the darkness.

Andy and Johannes continued their work on the X Flare although Andy tied the flaps of the tent back so he could keep line of sight with me where I sat on my roll mat, binoculars firmly clasped in my hands. As soon as it was light enough, I focussed on the top of the cliff, breath held and every muscle tense as I waited for the shock of seeing Bineshii.

Who was gone.

Of course he was gone. No-one would spend all night standing on a cliff edge staring into the darkness. I let out a sigh of relief as I scanned the ledge, searching for any sign.

"He's gone!" I called to Andy who hastened out, training the second pair of binos on the cliff.

"Bastard." he muttered before frowning "Hey, the rope's gone too!"

He was right. The anchored climbing line was no longer flapping in the breeze. From this distance it was too far to see if the anchor was still held in the wall and I swore, wondering what on earth could have happened.

A shout from the treeline, close to the camp and Andy brought his rifle up, moving into cover behind the stack of crates.

"See anything?" he called to me, a second later. I was still sitting, frantically bringing my rifle to bear and I stared at the treeline but almost immediately saw Martin's form, running from between the trees.

Followed by Gibbo and the others, all running far too slowly for men of their physical fitness as though they were slowed by sand or boggy ground.

"They've got a stretcher." Andy suddenly realised and I focused the binos, staring at the makeshift basha they had suspended between them on which a pair of feet rested, revealing the man who lay prone.

"Get the med kit!" I shouted unnecessarily as Andy grabbed the nearest bag marked with a red cross. He bullied Johannes out of the tent, laying a bed roll down to take the casualty before he sprinted out to meet Martin and add his strength to drag the stretcher close.

But as they ducked awkwardly under the guide wire there was no mad dash for the med kit or the makeshift hospital bed. Instead they dropped the stretcher unceremoniously to the cold ground and whirled around, rifle barrels pointing in every direction, faces whiter and more shaken than any man who claimed the distinction of a serving SAS soldier had any right to be.

I rolled onto my front, wincing at the pain and crawled on my belly, dragging my crutches and rifle with me to see the casualty. When I reached it, I reeled back in horror, fumbling for my own weapon and mirroring the actions of the soldiers, staring around for the enemy, the hidden predator who had done this to one of our own.

Beside me, the headless corpse lay unmoving on the stretcher.

*

After some time, we were still alive and there seemed no imminent chance of attack. Everyone calmed down a degree although from the twitching eyes that never stopped swivelling and the muted tones we spoke in it was plain that fear still gripped us.

"Who is it?" I dared to ask as the corpse was impossible to identify. Or so I thought.

"Jeff." Martin grunted.

"How can you tell?"

He pointed and I saw that wrapped around his hips was a climbing harness and the longer I looked, the more I recognised before I realised that it was indeed Jeff.

The funny, silver haired man who looked more like a granddad than an SAS trooper. I shook my head, wondering who or what had been in those woods that could get the better of the sturdy warrior from my memory.

"Well?" I demanded as Martin crouched, rifle still facing outwards.

"Well, what?"

"We can't just cower here all day! Jeff's dead but Solly and Doug are still out there! Someone took that line down in the night, too."

"What?"

I passed him the binos as Gibbo came to crouch with us, staring up at the rock face. He shook his head, his colour bad.

"We need to get up there, Mar." he murmured.

"It's those bastard natives." grated Martin "You said you'd met them before?"

Gibbo shook his head, his tone cool for once "Nah. Heard about them though. There's nothing about them that'd make me think they did this though."

Martin didn't turn away from the forest but his body was lined with fury "Exactly who else do you think did this, Gibbo? There's us here and then them. No-one else. Us and a boat load of Gold." He shot a poisonous look at Johannes who, despite everything was still working on the X Flare.

Gibbo said nothing but I could see the tension on his face "We still need to get up there."

Martin exhaled, controlling his emotion and nodded. He called the others around and explained that they were going to try and follow Jeff's tracks.

"What about blood?" Andy asked "Was he beheaded where you found him?"

Martin blinked and I realised that he didn't know. It was a blunder and he knew it, looking away from Andy as Gibbo shook his head "No. Ground was dry. His neck's dry, too. He was beheaded and then dumped."

"Should be pretty easy to track then." Andy surmised "Whoever it was had to carry old Jeffster back here and he's a lump, even without his head."

No-one could argue with that and so Martin led them off again after scooping the basha from under Jeff. I tried to avoid looking at the stump where his head had been but Andy called me over after extracting a pair of blue gloves from the med kit.

"Sorry about this, mucker." he muttered to the headless corpse before beginning to examine the skin "See here? Smooth cut. Suggests a sharp blade did this in one swing." he pulled flesh away from the white stub of bone "Spine has been sliced between these two vertebra. That means it was a precision blow."

"An axe?" I suggested.

He nodded slowly, not looking away from the skin "Maybe. Something heavy to get through it. I've never seen someone beheaded so cleanly."

"You've seen a few?" I asked, my discomfort making my mouth babble.

Andy shot me a significant look and I bit down hard to stop myself talking. Stupid question.

"In medieval times they beheaded people and I know it usually took more than one stroke." he looked up at me to see the surprise on my face "I like history." he explained "The neck is a tough place to cut through. It's easy enough to cut a throat or sever an artery but the muscle and bone are tougher. That's why the French came up with the guillotine."

The odds of a functioning guillotine being out here in the wilderness were not worth mentioning and I told him.

"I know. I'm just saying that's the only thing I can think of that would get through the neck like this." He removed the gloves, carefully depositing them in a clinical waste bag and sealing it.

"No animals?" I asked, already knowing the answer "Bears?"

"Not a chance." he shook his head, pulling a spare tarp over Jeff "Nope. I think this was human."

"The Headless Valley." I muttered and Andy nodded.

"Someone's idea of fun. I suppose those natives really do want the Gold after all!"

Johannes had emerged from the tent without either of us noticing "They can't have it! Don't care how many heads they chop off. Bastards! Said we should've left them behind, boss!" he spat.

"We did leave Bineshii behind." I pointed out "How did he follow us?"

Andy shrugged "The other two? Too much of a coincidence that they up and vanish and then all this happens." he stared at the trees for a moment "I wouldn't want to be them if Gibbo gets his hands on them."

"I'd like to get my hands on them." I swore, furious at the injustice of the murder "They must have lost it to be attacking us like this."

"What do you mean?" Andy asked.

"Like, the SAS." I explained, the fact seeming obvious to me "The best soldiers in the world, armed to the teeth and they're really going to try and fight us?"

"I'm glad you're so confident." Andy murmured.

"Aren't you?"

In response, he indicated Jeff "He was a top bloke, as good as any of us despite his age. Those native blokes we met were all old, pudgy and didn't look like they had a violent bone in their body. Plus, Jeff was killed by beheading. Do you see any of those blokes managing to swing an axe?"

I admitted that I did not. I also pointed out that Andy's words were far from helpful at which he grunted.

"... check... check..." an unexpected burst of human voice from the radio which Andy snatched up at once.

"Go ahead, over."

Static.

"You're unreadable. Say again, over."

"..."

"Bloody radios." Andy swore "I hate bloody radios."

The static faded until there was nothing. We both stared in the direction Martin and the others had gone, willing our eyes to see through the thick undergrowth.

"Keep an eye on the cliff, will you?" Andy asked after a few minutes and turned to help Johannes with the repairs.

I kept the binos scanning over the forest and back towards the cliff face. No eerie faces loomed over the cliff at me which was a relief. No soldiers scaled the rocks either, which was not.

A sudden burst of Afrikaans from Johannes and an

appreciative whoop from Andy. I managed to limp over to the tent, leaning heavily on my crutch to see Johannes turning a screwdriver as rapidly as his wrist would allow.

"What?" I demanded.

"He's bloody fixed it!" Andy was beaming as though one of his friends did not lay beheaded outside "The man's a genius!"

"Not as bad as I thought, boss." Johannes sounded apologetic but was still grinning "Sorry, it's the first time I've used the machine."

"Doesn't matter!" I enthused "Is it ready?"

"Yah." He grinned, standing up "Come on, we've got lost time to make up for!"

Manoeuvring it down to the water made both men pour with sweat and by the time it was in the shallows, Andy was bending to scoop the ice cold river water up and soak his head with it.

"Bloody thing –"

We all whipped around, eyes wide and staring as the unmistakeable chatter of machine gun fire erupted from the woods.

CHAPTER 16

I tried to drop flat, not easy when one leg refuses to bend and so I crashed onto the rocks deposited by the river, bruising the entire left side of my body and drawing blood from my wrist. I could have cared less.

"Where is it?" I hissed at Andy who had taken a kneeling position, his well-trained eyes scanning for the source of the fire.

"Way off." He muttered and reached out a hand for the binoculars which I passed him.

"Anything on the cliff?"

"No."

A second burst of fire, this one supported by tightly grouped rifle shots echoed off the canyon walls.

"Balls." muttered Andy.

"That's the Minimi."

"Yeah. And the rifles are five-five six. Definitely Martin."

"Maybe they saw a bear?" I suggested but more fire sounded, followed by the unmistakeable concussion of a grenade.

"Jesus wept." Andy snapped. He stood and began to run towards the camp where the weapons were cached but paused, half turning to Johannes and I.

"Get in some cover and –"

The sound of the bullet striking his body was like a high pitched *zip* sound followed by a meaty thud. I felt warm liquid splatter my face and Andy went flying forwards as though he'd been hit by a car. A second later the report of the rifle, strangely muffled, filled my ears and vibrated the walls of the canyon.

"Shit!" Johannes swore and I turned to see him crawling

through the shallows, soaked once again as he grabbed Andy, dragging him back out of the open towards one of the boats. Blood filled the water around him and I was grateful I'd fallen flat, not daring to think who of the three of us would make the easier target if I'd remained standing.

"Help me!" hissed Johannes and I half rolled towards him as he pulled Andy towards the closest boat, using the hull as cover.

"Did you see where it came from?"

"The trees! Where else?"

Together, still pressed to the ground we managed to lever Andy over the side of the boat and unceremoniously let him fall the short distance into the bottom of the hull before Johannes took a deep breath and launched himself with surprising agility over the side, landing with a thump next to Andy.

Zip

CRACK

The shot cut the air above my head and I heard a whimper, pressing myself down onto the cold stones, cringing away from the sniper.

"Johannes!"

"All good, boss." The grizzled Gold hunter knocked on the hull of the boat next to my head "Best you don't come up though, eh?"

I agreed, fervently before I remembered Andy "Is he alright?"

There was a pause, some shuffling "Nope."

"How bad?"

"One less share of the Gold type of bad, boss."

I cursed. The friendly man had been such a towering bastion of skill and training a moment before and now he was dead.

"Where was he hit?" I felt numb as I asked the question, wanting mostly to fill the silence.

"Chest. Big bullet, too."

"Like the rifles the hunters had?"

"Mmm. Could be. You hear the shot though?"

I thought back, shaking a little from the cold ground. The crack of the rifle had sounded a little odd and I mentioned it.

"Suppressed. That rifle the big boss had was silenced, wasn't it?"

I recalled the weapon Gibbo had snatched up last night. Now I thought about it, the barrel had seemed an odd shape and I felt a shudder of terror run through me at the thought that someone was using our own weapons against us.

Or some*thing*.

"Boss? You alright?"

"Yeah. Just cold."

A rustling sound and then Johannes tossed Andy's coat to me. Blood soaked it but I forced myself to ignore it, pulling the thick layer over me.

Zip

CRACK

A third bullet, this one close enough for me to imagine I felt the air from its passage strike my face and I went totally still.

"Suppressed, boss. For sure. Almost certainly military."

I swore. There wasn't much else to do.

"I vote we stay still until it gets dark." Johannes' voice came from the boat "Then we get out in the river and we anchor until daylight. Sound good?"

"Yeah."

"Want to know something good, boss?"

I agreed that I would and Johannes chuckled.

"The Gold is all in this boat."

I tried to laugh but just couldn't manage it.

We stayed still for hours as Andy's body cooled just inches from my head. The rocky ground was excruciatingly uncomfortable and I felt tingling sensations in my spine as blood was squeezed from vital muscles. I made small movements, trying to focus on forcing life back into the numb areas, remembering the long hours I'd spent stood on parades back in the HAC. Now the months of war, monotonous as they'd been seemed like a familiar memory, far preferable to the nightmare I now found myself in. There was some irony in the fact that in the months I'd spent 'at war' I'd never once heard a shot fired in anger and now here I was on 'holiday' with a dead friend next to me and the strong possibility that I'd be next. I wondered what part of our actions had drawn the ire of the natives so strongly that they'd want us dead. Had we disrespected the river? Failed to pay homage to some unknown deity? If so, why hadn't they told us? Gibbo had ensured that we were respectful to them and we'd willingly shared our camp and hospitality. The two men who'd stayed, Niimi and John had seemed friendly enough, although taciturn, but to imagine them as murderers was a stretch and to see them successfully taking out two, or maybe more SAS soldiers required such mental gymnastics that my mind began to spiral obsessively about the nature of our unseen enemy.

"You good, boss?"

"Living the dream."

"I'm doing some thinking here..." Johannes sounded pensive.

"You and me both." I hissed, then wondered why I was whispering when the shooter knew exactly where we were.

"See, if it's those natives that's shooting us here, I got to wonder *why?*"

I nodded, then remembered Johannes couldn't see me "That's what I was thinking."

For some reason, that made Johannes snort "Right. So, you got any ideas?"

"Maybe we disrespected them?"

Johannes thought about it "Maybe. But disrespect and them killing us is a big stretch, boss."

"The Gold, then?"

"Right!" Johannes sounded as enthusiastic as ever at the mention of the yellow metal "They've seen we're pulling it out and they want a piece."

"But..." I trailed off, thinking "But we aren't getting that much on this trip."

"Gonna get enough!" Johannes argued.

"Right. But not enough to murder ten men."

"I seen crazier things happen." Johannes spat inside the boat.

I wasn't buying it and I told him which made him silent for

a moment. I listened to the churning of the river and the wind between the rock faces but there was no more sound of gunfire.

"If it's not them, what is it?" Johannes asked.

I didn't like that word 'what' and I asked him what he meant.

"We had that whistling, now we've got a dead man with no head, cut through like a guillotine."

"What are you saying?" if there was anger in my voice it was because I didn't want such thoughts in my head. The very real threat of the sniper was frightening enough without some supernatural apparition.

"I'm saying, boss, one plus one equals two. And you can't tell me that headless body makes any sort of sense."

"No." I agreed "Andy said you'd need an axe to get through the neck like that."

"He said axe and a big strong swing. None of those natives were strong enough to do that. Not whilst Jeff was still alive."

"Urgh." I groaned "This isn't helping us, Johannes."

"Nothing's gonna help us except darkness." he pointed out "I'm just trying to prepare for what comes then."

"You mean the whistling?"

"Right."

"You think we'll be safer on the river?"

"I think we'll be safer back in Fort Simpson but whilst those boys are still out there, we've got ourselves a chance at getting this Gold back. And the fewer of us there are, the more we each get to keep."

I shuddered, remembering Adam's warning back in London. I didn't think that Johannes was going to go so far as to commit murder but the undeniable relish in his tone sent shivers through me that had nothing to do with the drop in temperature.

"We don't have any food." I pointed out.

Johannes made no comment to that. There wasn't any argument and so he was silent again for a short while.

"You still got those binos, boss?"

"Hang on." I checked, finding to my surprise that they were

still attached to me by the strap. I'd forgotten about them in the hurry to seek cover.

"Can you see the cliff?"

It seemed madness to move but I was behind the boat and well covered by the squat outline of the hull so I risked moving my head, finding to my surprise that I had a clear line of sight to the rock face that had held the severed rope. I quickly trained the binos, remembering a half second later the mystery shooter in the treeline and found myself torn between the two targets.

"See anything?"

"Looking for the sniper."

Johannes scoffed "He'll be way back in the trees."

"Still…"

But there was nothing to be seen. If the mystery shooter still lurked beneath the green canopy, then they were well concealed. Instead, I turned my vision to the cliff face, the sight of which I was fast beginning to loathe.

"There's a rope!" and there was. Two ropes in fact, both firmly anchored to the rock judging by their tautness. I scanned the cliff face for a sign of life but despite the cord moving gently in the faint breeze, there was nothing. No dour faced native surveying me from the top, no bold SAS team scrambling up with vengeance in their hearts and no mysterious, head chomping, whistling monster.

"So, they went back up?" Johannes guessed "What about all that shooting?"

"That was definitely in the woods." I remembered "But they must have gone up the cliff after that."

"So, we think they're still alive." Johannes reasoned and I felt a surge of relief at his words.

"But won't the sniper get them when they come back?"

"Hmm. Maybe he'll hold fire when he sees how many of them there are?"

"But the rifle was suppressed." I remembered "So maybe one of our guys was killed and the sniper got his weapon?"

The river gushed behind me as we both thought about it.

"Maybe there's another team." Johannes suddenly thought "Someone else got wind of our Gold expedition and came to claim it for themselves."

I started to rubbish the idea but a thought occurred to me that sent anger pulsing through my mind "Solly!" I hissed his name like a curse "He knew, didn't he? That's what all these weapons are for."

There was silence from within the boat as Johannes processed my words.

"He must have told someone about it or someone told him that we were being followed." I shook my head.

"Wouldn't he have just called the whole thing off?" Johannes wondered.

"No." months shut in that bunker in Europe had given me a deep insight into Solly's mind. A reasonable man in most situations, he was simply not the type to lose. If someone had challenged him by saying they were racing us to the Gold, he'd have risen to the bait.

"Why didn't he tell us?" I wondered.

To that, we had no answer. Not completely satisfied with the conclusions, I continued scanning the cliff face but to no avail. No more noises sounded and as the long, uncomfortable hours passed, we began to plan for the night ahead.

"We've got to anchor the boat." Johannes insisted "We can't ride the river in the dark and if we put the lights on –"

"We'll end up like Andy. Right." I nodded "The boats don't have anchors, do they?"

"No. We can make one out of the rope though."

I heard rustling as Johannes moved around in the bilge of the Raider. Suddenly he hissed "Got it! You know the other day when he tied that rope around his waist to jump in the river? It's still attached to the boat."

"Brilliant!" I hissed. Finally, a lucky break.

"Can you see any big rocks?"

I looked around. Most of the smaller stones I was lying on were fist sized, worn smooth by the action of the river and would not do. But a few metres away was a decent sized boulder that looked out of place, still rough edged as though it had fallen from the rock face that stood a hundred metres away.

"Got one."

"Alright."

We waited. The temperature dropped. Martin did not return. The sniper did not fire again. I began to obsess about how dark it was, wondering if I could still make out the treeline still or if it was just my imagination.

"Not yet." Johannes hissed.

"Nearly dark."

"Not yet." he repeated.

I began to shiver. Andy's blood had dried on the coat making the fabric stiff and I did my best to brush the brown stains off, flaking the smooth stones below me. Revulsion suddenly made me gag and in a flash of fear, I wondered what I was doing here and why I hadn't listened to Adam's advice back in London.

We didn't freeze overnight although I shivered through the hours of darkness as the boat bumped occasionally in the current, the anchor line holding us fast to the shore. The pitch blackness for once felt welcome and I relished the opportunity to sit up, stretching cramped muscles as Johannes moved Andy's corpse to the far end of the craft. A few moments later, he fell asleep.

I shook my head in disbelief as his light snores filled the hull, wondering at how he could relax in such circumstances. I tried to lie down but the bottom of the boat had water in it mixed with Andy's blood and I was cold so I shivered and tried not to give in to despair.

Peeeee-hoooo

The whistle split the night, coming from the shore just a few metres away. Johannes jerked awake, staring into the darkness.

Peeeee-hoooo

I grabbed my rifle, leaning it with shaking hands over the edge of the boat and pulled the trigger.

Click

The safety catch was still on. Cursing, I flicked it off with my thumb and fired.

Crack

Crack-crack-crack

A dim shape in the muzzle flash. Was it a person? I fired again.

Crack-crack-crack

Peeeee-hoooo

A pause. Stones clicked together on the beach. The river rushed past.

Twang

A new sound, followed by a jerk and the sudden sensation of movement as the anchor line was cut and we were plunged out into the pitch black of the current and the mercy of the fast flowing river.

CHAPTER 17

It was nothing short of a miracle that we didn't drown that night. My track record with the Nahanni was abysmal to say the least so I like to think that this was the river's way of giving me a break. Still, Johannes and I could do nothing but crouch in the bottom of the Raider as the craft swirled and twisted like a fairground ride, the hiss of approaching rapids bringing my heart into my mouth only for us to bump our way through them with luck that I'm sure we didn't deserve.

We drifted for what felt like hours but couldn't have been longer than forty minutes. Finally, I felt a grating crunch and I cringed for the inevitable rush of icy water and the drowning I was sure would follow but instead the mad swirling motion stopped and boat appeared to be still.

"You alright, boss?" Johannes called in a low voice.

"Yeah. Can you see what we're caught on?"

"No. I'm going to risk a torch."

Part of me wanted nothing more than to hide in the darkness but it might be that we needed to exit the boat in a hurry or, haul it further onto whatever protrusion we'd caught on before the Nahanni dragged us off again.

The stab of blinding white light flashed on, dazzling me and I closed my eyes to slits instinctively, straining to see what I could. Instantly, I could tell we had moved downstream of our camp. We were in a different section of the canyon altogether and I vaguely recognised it from the journey upstream. A small pebbly beach had our keel fast although it was no more than five metres in depth and was backed by sheer walls.

"Quick!" Johannes leapt from the boat onto the tiny spit, grabbing the side of the hull to steady it as I patted around me to find the severed anchor line. Sopping wet rope met my hands and I hauled it in, finding that it had been cut at its furthest extremity meaning there was plenty to toss to Johannes.

Not a moment too soon either because as his weight had left the boat it had risen and the current was moving us again and I hollered at him to hold it fast, finally finding the control for the floodlights and dazzling us in the brilliant glow.

"Here!" Johannes found a rock similar to the one we'd used to anchor earlier and in a trice, had the rope secured. I breathed a sigh of relief, painfully levering myself out of the boat onto the spit of beach.

"Kill the lights?" he suggested and I nodded, watching as he reached over to dim the glow and we settled down on the pebbles, glad to finally be out of the wild current.

"How far do you think we came?" I asked, rubbing my hands together for warmth.

"A mile? Two?" he was guessing. In the pitch blackness it was impossible to tell.

"How can we risk going back in the morning with that sniper still there?"

He blew air out of his cheeks as he realised the perils of such an endeavour. As we approached the beach the shooter would be able to pick us off with ease, effectively barring our return to camp.

"We need to get back." I reasoned "We can't get down the river without food and we'd have to ditch Andy's body anyway." The health risks of travelling next to a corpse for multiple days were obvious and I winced at the idea of dumping him in the river.

Peeeee-hoooo

"The hell?" Johannes leapt to his feet, staring around in the darkness as I fumbled for my rifle.

"The torch!" I snapped, anger rising in me. Now the threat of the sniper was gone I was ready to find the whistling beast and fill it with as much lead as I could shoot.

Brilliant light stabbed the darkness, roving over the cliff faces, the dark water and the boat.

Nothing moved, save the churning Nahanni.

"Up there!" Johannes suddenly directed the beam at the cliff face above us and we both staggered towards the boat as a small tumble of rocks fell where we'd been standing. I leaned hard on Johannes, cursing my broken leg and stared as he shone the torchlight back up.

"Show your face!" I bawled at the now empty cliff "Come on! Come and have a go!"

Nothing moved.

"There's a cave." Johannes had leaned back further to see above us, his boots getting wet in the process.

"How high?"

"Ten metres?" he guessed.

"There's something in the caves." I swore, realising that the woods had not been the source of our mysterious stalker. I remembered from my research that the cave networks were extensive and almost completely unmapped. For all we knew they led up to the top of the cliffs and explained how the natives had been able to vanish so effectively.

Peeeee-hoooo

"Fuck off!" I snarled as Johannes activated the boat lighting again, staring around. I raised the rifle, sighting on the cave mouth but there was nothing to see and I couldn't risk another rock fall.

"Should we go up?" Johannes asked.

"No chance I can get up there." I was sitting on the hull of the boat, my leg stretched out before me.

"I reckon I can."

I stared, but Johannes was already standing at the foot of the rocks, placing his hands tentatively in a couple of spots for handholds. Suddenly, with a grunt of effort he raised himself up, using his legs to push. Surprisingly agile, Johannes was six feet up the wall in a couple of steps, hands testing for a new hold as I leaned back, pointing both the torch and the rifle at the cave above us.

Peeeee-hoooo

"Definitely the cave!" I shouted and Johannes gave a snarl, moving up until he was almost below the lip of the dark entrance.

Peeeee-hoooo

Peeeee-hoooo

Peeeee-hoooo

Fear gripped me and I clenched my jaw in response, twitching the rifle barrel left and right. Johannes' jacket had fallen open and I could make out the holstered handgun he must have filched from Solly's stores.

Peeeee-hoooo

Peeeee-hoooo

Peeeee-hoooo

The sound was fading as though whatever it was had moved off through the cave.

"It's leaving!" I shouted as Johannes finally got his right hand to the lip of the rock, then his left and then swung himself up, immediately scrabbling to draw the pistol.

"Throw the torch!" he shouted and I cursed, realising in our haste, he'd left me with the only light. I took a deep breath, letting the rifle hand by its sling and tossed the small device, watching as it sailed end over end, finally clattering on the rock where Johannes pounced it like a man in a desert finding water. He shone it forward, pointing the barrel of the stolen pistol into the depths of the opening.

"What's there?" I shouted, desperate for an answer.

Which Johannes didn't give. Instead, he called down that he was going in and stepped forward, ducking into the narrow space and he was gone.

I stared up, seeing the glow from the torch illuminate the cave entrance and slowly fade as Johannes moved further inside.

Peeeee-hoooo

My heart nearly froze as the whistle came from the river. I wheeled around, pointing the rifle wildly.

Peeeee-hoooo

"Where are you?" I snarled and in the glow of the boat lights saw movement on the cliffs the far side of the flowing Nahanni.

I emptied the rifle magazine, firing almost blind but hearing the rounds strike small stones from the rock face.

"Boss!" Johannes called down.

"Opposite side!" I snapped, changing magazines as fast as I could and covering the rock face with the muzzle again. Johannes shone the torch but the thin beam couldn't reach across the fast water.

Cursing, I grabbed the nearest floodlight and began turning it, forcing the stiff bearing to rotate until it shone on the opposite cliff.

Nothing.

Peeeee-hoooo

Far away now, high above us. I tried to move the light but I wouldn't bend that way. I heard a stream of swearing from above me.

"I'll go look inside here a bit more, boss." Johannes declared "It's messing with us!"

What was it? What animal could possibly move in such a way? Unless there was more than one.

I shivered.

Peeeee-hoooo

Definitely at the top of the canyon now, moving away. Johannes' light had vanished now, he was already deep inside the cave. I looked around, doing my best to keep my head on a swivel and jumped out of my skin as I saw Andy, lying dead in the bows of the boat. I'd completely forgotten him in the adrenaline and I leaned back, hand over my heart.

"Sorry, pal." I muttered to the lifeless corpse, only after I said it realising how mad it was to talk to a dead man. I sneered at my own foolishness, trying to get a grip of the fear that was burning through me. No more whistling sounds came although my heart rate didn't drop a bit.

"Boss?"

118

Johannes was back and I looked up at him.

"You alright?"

"All good. There's nothing here, no tracks, no nothing."

"How far does the cave go?"

"A long way. I hit a couple of junctions and didn't want to get lost. It might go all the way to the top."

"There was one the other bank, too. That means there's more than one of these things."

"Boss, the caves are easily big enough for a man. I don't think this is anything but the natives messing with us. Hold on –"

He swung himself back down the short rock face with apparent ease, landing back on the small beach with me.

"They clearly followed us on the river and if they're on both sides they can use the caves to get up and down. That whistle must be something they made to communicate or to scare the bejesus out of us."

"Like an elk whistle?" I suddenly remembered the hunting tools I'd seen used on a deer stalk in the UK.

"Yeah! Maybe." Johannes was nodding "Bloody natives, scaring the piss out of us!"

It all began to make sense. The gunfire in the woods, the stolen sniper rifle. Clearly, the three men we'd met were part of a much larger group and were doing their best to ambush the SAS team and pick us off one by one. I wondered at the apparent ease with which they moved and guessed we were not the first group they had intimidated.

"But probably the most stubborn." Johannes pointed out.

"Right. We're tooled up. Maybe that's what Solly was worried about?"

"I don't know about that." Johannes was wary "Still, we've got to get back to the camp."

"Right." I thought about it for a minute "How about we keep close to the rock face and try to anchor behind one of those bigger boulders?"

Johannes racked his brains trying to remember the rocks in the water near our camp. I thought I remembered some enormous chunks of stone that had fallen from the cliff face and now protruded from the water, big enough to hide the boat behind but now I thought about it, I wondered if my memory was wrong.

"I think there were." The South African frowned in the glare of the spotlights.

"We'll have to try."

The whistling natives left us alone the rest of the night. Perhaps they thought they'd scared us off. I even managed to get some sleep although Johannes curiously didn't drop off, instead crouching with his borrowed pistol until the grey light of dawn reached us and we started the boat engine, setting off up the river at the slowest pace we could manage, hugging the rock faces and keeping our heads on a swivel. As fear gripped me, I bared my teeth, fed up with being stalked and teased. Whoever this enemy was, I was done being scared of them. I'd come here for Gold and damn it, I was going to leave with some. Then we'd get back to civilisation and let the authorities deal with the whole sorry mess. The thought of them being slammed in prison gave me a grim satisfaction and I nodded to myself as we swept through the gloomy canyon.

CHAPTER 18

The boulders in the water were more than ample to shelter us as we swept around the final bend. I edged the boat closer as Johannes, my rifle slung over his shoulder grabbed the anchor line, preparing to hold us fast.

"Over there!"

The voice rang out over the churning of the water, a clear English accent and I jumped, the wheel twitching in response. I nudged the nose of the Raider around the boulder to see a cluster of men in rugged combat gear standing on the shore between the two other boats. I recognised Gibbo at once, the minimi hefted in his hands and blood across one cheek.

Relief coursed through me and I shoved the throttle wide, swinging the bows of the boat around and grounding it hard on the small beach.

"Solly!" I shouted, surprise and pleasure at seeing the man alive filling me. He nodded, his expression grim as Johannes and I leapt from the boat.

"Where's Andy?" was the question on everyone's lips and I gestured wordlessly to the boat.

"What happened?" Solly had grime around his eyes, suggesting he'd rubbed mud into his skin. He looked exhausted but his eyes were hard and I wondered at his tale.

"The sniper."

"Sniper?" Gibbo was close at hand, reaching over to check Andy's pulse despite the fact that the corpse was already beginning to give off a clear odour of decay.

I briefed Solly on the events of the previous night, the

suppressed rifle rounds, Andy's death and the whistling.

"You went into the cave?" Gibbo demanded of Johannes who blinked at the bigger man's tone before turning slightly so that he faced Gibbo down.

"Yeah." he grunted "So what?"

"Was that before or after Andy died?"

"Weren't you listening, eh? Hours after!"

"We think the natives have a way through the caves." I explained "That's how they're getting around us so easily."

"The natives?" Solly looked suspicious "Did you see them?"

I admitted we hadn't. I told him of the vague shapes I'd shot at in the darkness "That reminds me." I looked at Gibbo "Who were you shooting at?"

"How do you know I was shooting?" he demanded. I was taken aback by the tone. I'd avoided Gibbo as much as possible thus far, unable to contain my dislike of the man but even so, he looked as though he were one step away from levelling the Minimi at me. I glanced at Solly to see the same hard expression on his face.

And on all the others.

The others...

"Where's Martin?" I suddenly realised he was missing.

"Same place as Robbie." grunted Colin, gesturing towards the forest "Their bodies are in there. Any time you see their heads lying around you let us know."

I stared. Martin and Robbie were dead?

"How do you know I was shooting?" Gibbo stepped forward, pressing his ugly face into my personal space. I tottered on my crutches.

"Because there's only one machine gun in this godforsaken hell hole and last we saw it had your bloody great mitts all over it!" Johannes snapped, stepping between Gibbo and I.

"Or, you were the bastards helping those natives to slot Martin and Robbie last night!" Gibbo shoved Johannes hard so the older man staggered and fell onto the rocky shore "Wanted a bigger cut of the gold, did you? That's why they killed Andy!" he turned and shouted at the rest of the group. Our group. Our friends. I stared at Solly pleadingly.

"Andy was shot by a suppressed rifle firing from those trees!" I tried to keep my tone reasonable "We thought it was the one Colin took yesterday."

"This one?" Colin raised the rifle and I gaped at it.

"I think we know what happened here." Gibbo stepped forward, boot raised to kick Johannes who was sprawled in a sitting position, hands behind him.

"Bastard." he snarled as Gibbo swung his boot towards him.

What happened next was so fast no-one had time to react. Johannes, with a speed I'd never have thought possible went for the knife he concealed in his belt. He was on his feet, blade driving upwards towards Gibbo before I'd even registered that he was moving. I stared in horror, fully expecting yet another death but Gibbo, foul mouthed, snarling Gibbo who'd bullied and belittled us as recruits earning our hatred forever whipped the knife from Johannes' hand with all the speed of a striking viper and rammed the blade into the South African's eye socket.

I don't know if there was a gasp of shock. In my memory there is but it all happened so fast I could be wrong. I could see Solly's eyes were wide with shock as the scene unfolded before him. The others had taken steps forward but no-one was close enough to stop Gibbo who snarled in a victory grimace as Johannes collapsed like a wet towel, cracking his head against the smooth stones, the hilt of his own knife protruding from his eye.

The other eye stared up sightlessly as death rattled in his throat.

"What the fuck!" I snarled, raising my crutch at Gibbo. What was happening? The world had lost all sense and I was briefly aware that Solly was moving to step between us as Gibbo turned his murderous face on me when, in true vindication, the hidden sharpshooter saved my life and shot Gibbo in the back.

Zip

CRACK

There was no mistaking the sound and last night's experience sent me flat to the stones again, landing beside Johannes. Blood was leaking from some part of him and I felt sick at his death. But Gibbo had fallen against the boat I'd just landed on the beach and was on his knees gasping and grunting.

"Treeline!" Solly had shouted but it was unnecessary because the rest of the group was now shredding the forest with gunfire, tearing bark from trunks and needles from branches.

"Liam!" he snarled and I rolled across the hard stones to a position I could fire from. Levelling the rifle, I fired rounds as fast as my finger could pull the trigger without knowing who or what I was firing at.

Colin suddenly shouted from the ground where he was out of my line of sight "Two knuckles left of shoreline! Base of tree! Watch my shots!" he then fired with the scoped rifle and I saw the distinctive chunk of white wood as the heavy round struck the tree.

I changed my magazine and emptied it into the undergrowth as the others did the same.

"Moving!" it was the only sound that the professionals shouted as they began the process of leapfrogging forward. Solly, Colin and Doug bounding towards the unseen enemy as I remained with the wounded Gibbo who was giving off awful sounds.

I heard a scream from the treeline, saw Doug had already closed the short distance and had abandoned his rifle for his handgun and was moving in a steady diagonal line, firing shot after shot at something on the ground before him.

"Coming back!"

The three of them were running back with Solly and Doug dragging a corpse between them.

A corpse dressed in tactical gear with a heavy barrelled rifle that Colin now clutched, almost identical to his own.

But not a native and certainly not an SAS soldier.

"Who is that?" I shouted to Solly but he shoved me aside, running to treat Gibbo as Colin and Doug faced outwards, giving us the protection of their rifle barrels.

"Who is he?" I demanded, staring at the dead man who was

white skinned, thirty something and sported a hefty beard. Blood soaked his gear which was modern and high quality. He looked like an enemy soldier. But from which army?

Gibbo gave another groan and I turned, unable to feel any pity for Johannes' murderer. Solly had the body armour off and was examining the skin which appeared to be unbroken. I felt a surge of disappointment that the miserable ex-PSI was going to survive but as I watched he coughed and blood spattered the skin of his face.

"How is he?" Colin shouted back and I reported the blood. Doug swore and wriggled back on his belt buckle to examine Gibbo as Solly took his place in the defensive formation.

Adrenaline killing the pain in my leg, I crawled up next to Solly, nudging him in the ribs "Oi. Tell me what's going on. Right bloody now."

He looked at me shrewdly "No."

"Screw you, Solly! You didn't bring all this kit with you for some light sport shooting, did you? Are you even here for the Gold?"

"No." Colin replied as Solly shot him a dangerous look "What? You may as well tell him, Sol. It's only fair." there was a pause before Colin continued "Either that or shoot him."

I stared but the man was deadly serious. I looked back to see Solly staring at me with a predatory gleam in his eyes and I felt a stab of fear.

"Don't shoot me! We're all on the same side here, aren't we? What's so bloody secret that you can't tell me? Remember I'm a soldier in the same army you are!"

There was silence. Behind us Gibbo gave a groan.

"How is he, Dougie?" Solly called, ignoring me for a moment.

"Bad." was the perfunctory reply "Internal bleeding. The round didn't break the skin but the armour seems to have made the impact worse. I can't treat this, Sol. We need to casevac him right now."

Gibbo spat and choked before we all heard his hissing voice "I'm fine! You get these wankers that killed our blokes! You do that..." his voice faded and I looked around to see Doug had injected him with something, Gibbo had gone slack and I guessed he had been sedated. Doug looked over at Solly.

"We aren't shooting the STAB, Sol."

A surge of gratitude washed over me.

"It's not his fault. We don't have to tell him everything, either." Doug looked hard at me "He just has to follow orders."

"Speaking of orders." Colin looked significantly at Solly "Are we bugging out?"

Solly looked like a man on the edge of madness. Exhaustion lined his face and the grief he must have felt at his comrades' death was no doubt weighing him down. Colin was equal to his boss though and held the man's gaze.

I saw movement at the edge of my vision. Instinct from long hours spent scrutinising the vista before me made me jerk around to look and I saw the men in the treeline.

"Contact!" I yelled as the first rounds sounded.

"Colin!" shouted Solly, a meaning in his voice that I couldn't guess at but Colin nodded and a moment later had removed a cylindrical device from his kit and fired it in a small parabolic arc.

BOOM

The grenade shot smoke into the trees and voices cried out in confusion.

"Let's do it!" Solly roared and Colin shot a second, then a third into the trees and suddenly Solly was up, racing forwards in a mad charge across the open ground. I felt Doug pass me moving at a speed that would have a whippet whining in jealousy and then Colin was gone and I was once again on my belt buckle as around me the world tore itself to pieces.

CHAPTER 19

Peeeee-hoooo

The whistling was back. Darkness had fallen again on another long day spent in Headless Valley. Gibbo was unconscious next to me. Solly, Colin and Doug were dead for all I knew. They'd vanished into the trees and gunfire had raged for what felt like hours. Even now, long after the light had failed, I could hear sporadic shots.

I didn't dare to move. My bladder had filled and I'd emptied it into the stones, not caring if I laid in my own waste as I stared out at the treeline, cursing for the millionth time my broken leg. Without that, I told myself, I'd have torn after the others, throwing myself into the battle that had raged. Then I'd know what was happening, who the enemy was and what madness had driven me to believe that Solly had come here for Gold.

Because, as I lay there amidst the dead and dying, I realised how naïve I'd been. Adam had tried to warn me back in London at that smart table. He'd told me what happened when people caught Gold Fever. But then, whatever was happening with Solly was nothing to do with the Gold, surely? This was something else, something that was worth them seriously considering killing me over. Was I caught in some government conspiracy? Had Solly been sent here on a mission? Were the enemies the rival forces of some unknown nation, here to recover... what? The wreckage of a crashed UFO? A mysterious weapons package developed by a mad scientist in a hidden lab? Bigfoot? Every possibility was as unlikely as the last and I wished Johannes could talk to me.

I was hyper aware of his presence, just a couple of metres away lying on his back. It was odd, I had to keep reminding myself that he was dead but my mind wouldn't wrap around the concept. I kept thinking of things to say to him and actually opened my mouth to speak a handful of times, letting out the breath in a disappointed sigh.

Gibbo groaned.

I crawled back over to him, sympathy long having fled "What?" I demanded.

He wanted Fentanyl. I didn't care and told him so. That shut him up for a while as he realised he was at my mercy. But I wasn't him and I couldn't justify intentionally causing him harm. Besides, Doug had all the Fentanyl and statistically speaking he was now a headless corpse somewhere beyond the treeline.

"Solly didn't tell you, did he?" Gibbo's voice was strained, much like someone who has had the wind knocked out of them even though it was hours since he'd been shot.

"That you aren't here for Gold?"

"No... We are here for Gold. There's something else here too though."

"Well?" I snapped when he went silent.

"Don't ask." Gibbo's voice was a hiss "S'not worth knowing. Solly'll kill you if you know."

"For the love of God!" I was furious now. I considered prodding his ribs but worried such an action might kill the man "None of us are getting out of this at this rate. It's just you and me now. What's so secret I can't be told?"

I wondered if he had passed out. In any case, I got nothing out of Gibbo. Instead, Solly, Doug and Colin reappeared in the middle of the night, almost making me shoot them as they materialised out of the dark like ghosts, their faces smeared with mud. Solly directed the others to gather all the spare ammunition whilst he knelt by me.

Peeeee-hoooo

"What?" I demanded.

"Look mate, I'm sorry about earlier. There's a bigger picture here, Liam and I'm sorry you got deceived." before I could speak, I could sense him shaking his head "I know you want to know but it's above your paygrade and it's all gone tits up anyway. We're sitting ducks here on this beach and Gibbo needs hospital. First thing in the morning –"

Peeeee-hoooo

Right on top of us. The natives with their elk whistles?

Peeeee-hoooo

"Solly." I said in a tone of voice that was far calmer than it had any right to be "Just answer me one thing. I know you can't tell me, maybe you're on some unsanctioned super-ally mission, I don't know. Maybe you came here for Gold or maybe you just used a naïve STAB to get whatever the hell it is that you want, I can't tell. But just answer me this, Solly. Is that whistling part of it, or is it scaring the shit out of you too?"

Solly's silence was the single most frightening sound I'd ever heard. A rustle sounded next to me and I jumped, moving to aim my rifle but it was Colin's voice.

"No, mate. That's not part of the game."

Peeeee-hoooo

"So neither of you know what that is?"

Silence.

Peeeee-hoooo

Peeeee-hoooo

Peeeee-hoooo

Close at hand again. The eerie whistle of the Headless Valley.

Peeeee-hoooo

"There."

I saw movement. A figure, somehow distinct from the darkness that enveloped us. Colin and Solly were facing towards me, no doubt wrestling with their consciences and morals. I flicked off the safety catch on my rifle and fired at the shape.

A scream filled the night.

Peeeeeeeeeee-haaaaaaaaaaaaa

As though the whistle had been drawn out in a long shriek of agony.

Colin shot a flare into the air, heedless of incoming fire. There was a need that clutched all three of us now, a very human desire to understand the nature of our foe and to look our enemy in the eye.

We all saw the shape as it reached the treeline, still shattered from the gunfire and explosives earlier. A dark silhouette, four limbs, moving fast. That was all.

"What was that?" It was the inevitable question. I don't even know who asked it. At that moment Solly and Colin's years of training and expertise counted for exactly nothing. We were just three members of the same species, suddenly aware that something we could not explain had just happened.

"Was it human?"

"Had to be."

"Bear?"

As if to ridicule the suggestion, the screaming whistle split the night again.

Peeeeeeeeeee-haaaaaaaaaaaaa

"I shot the bastard at least." was there triumph in my voice? You're damned right there was.

Peeeeeeeeeee-haaaaaaaaaaaaa

Moving further away into the woodland, heading for the cliff face? Or vanishing into the caves.

"Is that what killed Martin and the others?" I asked.

"Yes." Solly's voice was devoid of emotion.

"But you don't know what it is."

"No."

I sighed "Brilliant. What do we do now?"

CHAPTER 20

What we did was wait for dawn. I was heartily sick of the sight of the grey canyon walls, the scattered remains of our camp and the gruesome image of the dead bodies.

As we moved carefully into the boat, I stared at the small pile of Gold dust we'd recovered. For a ticket out of here, I'd happily tip the lot back where it'd come from and fly home to London. I never wanted to see the Nahanni again as long as I lived, never wanted to venture outside the security of the M25. From now on an adventure would be taking the tube outside of zone one, perhaps spending my days riding to stations with funny names.

But more likely, I would rot here, a headless corpse in the Headless Valley.

The figure moved slowly out of the treeline, both arms held out to one side in the familiar NATO 'T' shape that signified a friendly soldier.

Every eye was drawn to him, every weapon suddenly trained.

"Shall I take him?" Colin had the man in his sights and I saw Solly's face twitch but he said nothing.

"No." I called, as if my voice held any weight but it must have done because Colin did not shoot.

The man approached slowly. As he came into focus, I could see the American flag on the front of his body armour, the distinctive shape of the HK416 rifle he carried and the Gatorz sunglasses that hung from a strap around his neck.

"Halt!" Colin snapped and the man stopped, his expression placid.

Solly had apparently abandoned all attempts at protocol

because he strode forward, coming to a halt next to where I lay on my belly "Who are you?"

"Lieutenant Nathaniel Jacobs. US Navy."

A dead silence. Even the river seemed to have paused, turning to stare in shock at this admission.

"This one of yours?" Solly indicated the corpse of the sniper, the one he and Colin had killed.

"No." Jacobs shook his head emphatically "That sonofabitch took out two of my guys though. Glad to see he got what was coming to him." Jacobs still held his arms out to the side.

"Put your rifle down." Colin instructed and Jacobs paused before slowly lowering the weapon to hang from its sling before him, pointedly not laying it down.

Solly made an introduction using a name and rank that were not his own. I could see Jacob's eyes narrow at the lie but he didn't argue. I wondered what his real name was.

"You're British SF?" he asked.

"And you're a Navy SEAL." Colin retorted.

The air between us was tense. After a second or two, Jacobs cracked a humourless smile "Last I checked, we were on the same side."

"Last I checked, this wasn't a conflict zone." Solly snapped.

"Right, and there weren't headless bodies lying around the woods?" Jacobs layered his tone with sarcasm "Look, I get it. We're all here for the same thing I'm assuming. I heard the legends about this place before we deployed, same as you did. I just didn't expect to lose half my guys killed to a damn mythical monster."

Solly didn't respond. Colin had his finger hovering around the trigger and behind me I guessed Doug was in a similar state. There was no way in hell that Jacobs had walked out here alone without a whole load of rifle barrels supporting him from the treeline and I was absolutely fed up with people trying to kill me.

I stood up with some difficulty.

"Liam Stryker, British Army Reserve." I introduced myself "These blokes are SAS. I brought them on a Gold hunting trip as extra muscle. Turns out you're all here for something else."

Jacobs raised an eyebrow at my unlikely.

"As it stands we've got four –" I glanced at Johannes body "-five dead blokes and one more on his way out. I don't know who that is –" I pointed at the dead sniper whose skin was already turning pale beneath the dried blood "I don't know why Navy SEALs are here and frankly, I couldn't give a toss. You say you've lost some men? As I see it, that puts us on the same side. I reckon you reached the same conclusion else you wouldn't have come walking out here." I leaned around him to look at the forest "Oi! Come on down! Plenty of food to go around!"

Solly snapped at me to stop behaving like a fool and I told him what he could do with his opinion. Jacobs repressed a smile.

"Things going about as well for you guys as they are for us!" he declared, turning around and waving his left hand over his head.

A half dozen soldiers emerged from the treeline. As I stared at them, I could see that they had been through hell. All were covered in dirt and blood, their equipment battered and deep bruises beneath their eyes.

"Seven of us total." Jacobs informed Solly who nodded. Colin stood up and slung his rifle as Doug stepped forward to ask if anyone needed a medic.

One of the SEALs, a chunky looking youth had a bullet wound on his thigh that looked serious and the ice broke as Doug began treating him. There was little chatter but I saw a few appreciative nods at the sight of the dead sniper.

"Was he alone?" I asked.

A SEAL snorted "Nope. A whole mess of them assholes came at us. Not many left now."

"How long have you been here?"

Jacobs eyed me shrewdly "We got here two days before you did."

"Did you bring boats?" I asked.

He shook his head "We jumped."

Colin frowned "Difficult landing, I bet."

"You're damn right it was." Jacobs spat "Most of our gear and food went into the river. Water is freakin' deep here."

I nodded, seeing the hunger on the men's faces "We have food."

They tore into the rations we had remaining, satiating a hunger that must have been racking them for days. After my night on the river with Johannes I was sympathetic. I was also no closer to finding out what on earth was going on here that required two of the west's premier fighting forces to deploy as though ready for a full scale war. I knew Jacobs wouldn't tell me and Solly was uncharacteristically quiet. Weirdly, I found that I didn't much care. There were far bigger problems at hand.

"Anyone hear that whistling?"

The SEALs snapped around to look at me and I saw the haunted look in their eyes.

"All night and all day." The man with the injured leg shook his head "Then we wake up and find someone else is missing their head. Goddamn."

"Get it together, Rubold." Jacobs snapped and the young man stiffened "Yessir."

"Did you see it?" I asked "The... *thing*?"

One said "No." another said "Kinda." And Rubold scowled.

"I saw a shape." I recalled "Thought it was one of the natives with an elk whistle."

"That wasn't an elk whistle." Jacobs declared "I've hunted for years. Zero chance that was a native."

"Natives don't jump up rock faces like that." another man cut in "And they don't go beheading goddamn SEALs!"

"Have you got comms with your base?" Solly asked but Jacobs shook his head.

"No. Can't get a signal, can't get anything. We knew this was a blackspot before we came in."

"You have a relief force?"

He shrugged "Not for another few days." He was deliberately vague, showing the limits of the trust between our two groups.

There was silence as the SEALs finished their meal and then Colin began distributing ammunition which was readily accepted. Colour began to return to the men's cheeks and I felt more than a little confidence return at the sight of the formidable force. A glance at Jeff's body quickly soured me though.

"So, did you find any Gold?" Rubold seemed to be a chatterbox, making light of the situation.

"Yep." I showed them, seeing their eyes light up at the sight of the yellow metal "Plenty more in there, too." I pointed at the fast flowing river.

"Goddamn." Rubold shook his head "So near but so far, huh?"

"Right." I agreed.

"Well –" he hefted his rifle, squatting down next to me on the rocky ground "- at least we might stand a chance of getting out of here now." He indicated the boats.

"We aren't leaving." Another SEAL, this one an older man with a thick beard and hard eyes growled.

Doug nodded his agreement "Now we know what's here, we can take it out. There's plenty of us now."

"We don't know *shit* about what's here!" I objected "All we know is there's two teams of guys who should be dominating this situation and instead we've got more bodies than we can fit on the boats!"

"Hey, asshole!" Jacobs shouted at me "Way to lighten the mood!"

I blinked, noticing the dejected expressions around me. I realised I'd made a bad break. Now was not the time for defeatism. I tried to make up for it.

"Well, what are we going to do?"

"Payback." the same SEAL who'd declared we weren't leaving was looking furious. A few of the others nodded.

"We need to make a plan." Solly seemed to have roused himself from the funk he was in danger of slipping into "Whatever it is, we haven't got a good look at it once." he pointed at the canyon walls "We think its using the caves to get around. Plus, there's the natives. We've been seeing them all around and if we can get hold of them, maybe they can tell us something."

"You guys came in with a couple of them." Jacobs sounded suspicious "You can't ask them?"

"They scarpered in the middle of the night." Doug shook his head "Our guess is they used the caves because that rock face is the only other way out of here.

"Maybe they had canoes?" Jacobs suggested but Solly shook his head.

"Didn't see any around."

A groan from Gibbo brought everyone's attention around. Doug hurried over to check on him as the man muttered something.

"What?" Solly called,

"He says we need to lay a trap." Doug called back.

"Right." Jacobs sounded enthusiastic "We lure it out here and light the sumbitch up."

"What about him?" I indicated the dead sniper "There were more of his team."

"Not in the woods." Jacobs declared "We cleared them on our way down here. Only way in and out is that rock face."

"So, we get it out in the open, blast some of these flares up and end it!"

There were murmurs of assent. Solly and Jacobs began marking out firing positions.

"You don't look happy." Rubold jibed.

I grimaced "We've been trying to fight this thing in the dark and its got us nowhere. We need to clear the caves."

He grunted "Can't argue with that. But this ambush might get us some of the answers we need."

What did I know? I was effectively a civilian next to these men. But logic dictated that we were not equipped to fight whatever it was that stalked us. I remembered the outline I'd seen in the darkness, the squat, ugly shape vanishing back into the treeline and felt my spirits fall.

"Maybe its bigfoot?" Rubold seemed excited at the idea.

I snorted "You know we shot it the other night? Heard it scream and everything."

"Aright!" Rubold clapped his hands together "If it can bleed, we can kill it, huh?"

I had to laugh. The thought of Arnold Schwarzenegger racing through this canyon with his ridiculous costume was so ridiculous I couldn't help it. The sound brought everyone's eyes onto us and more than a few eyebrows were raised. I felt some of the pressure of the past few days leave me and nodded to myself as I looked around at the bristling weapons that surrounded me. Maybe we'd be alright.

Peeeee-hoooo

Or maybe not.

CHAPTER 21

A tiny, sleep deprived, stressed and panicked part of my brain surged in relief that the noise had come in the light of day. A second later as the shouts and sharp movements of the massed SEALs and surviving SAS soldiers filled the air, I felt my stomach churn and my heart begin to pound. Remembering the bullets that had torn through the air above this very spot, I rolled onto the ground, once again pressing myself to the cold rocks that were beginning to feel like old friends.

Peeeee-hoooo

"Treeline!"

BOOM

I couldn't see what the weapon was – some form of explosive, clearly but one of the SEALs was frantically reloading and then a second explosion.

BOOM

I bared my teeth in a savage grin as the all too familiar sound of gunfire started again. I tried to look at the trees, seeing only a pall of smoke and a small fire, quickly spreading.

"Cease firing!"

The running of the river and the crackling of the flames. No other sound until we all let out the breaths we'd been jointly holding.

Peeeee-hoooo

Behind us now, every man turned to the river which gushed innocently.

Peeeee-hoooo

Peeeee-hoooo

Peeeee-hoooo

"There!" one of the SEALs, I hadn't caught his name was pointing across the flowing water to the opposite side of the canyon where caves rose far above the waterline.

"Where?"

He shouted complicated instructions trying to rely on his training to differentiate one cave from another but trailed off as the seconds passed.

"It was in a cave! I saw it move."

Jacobs stood, chopping his hand towards the far bank "Hit it!"

BOOM

The SEAL fired the explosive and we stared as if in slow motion as the missile shot across the river, impacting on the rock face. We were far enough from the shrapnel not to need to duck and so we saw in full detail as the rockface crumbled, pouring into the river and churning the water into white froth.

Peeeee-hoooo

Behind us now and I heard the snarls of frustration but the sound had changed and it came again.

Peeeee-hoooo

Peeeee-hoooo

Peeeee-hoooo

No longer the eerie shriek that had terrified us nor the wounded animal howl we'd heard as the rounds had struck home. Instead this was a call of alarm and as we turned, we saw why.

Fire.

The shattered leaves and branches that our gunfire had strewn across the treeline must have dried enough that the explosive had ignited them. A great pall of white smoke was already pouring upwards, blown away from us by the wind that gusted through the canyon. The closest trees were wrapped in a blanket of flame, the lower branches already blackened and dead as the green boughs whipped in the furnace wind like they were trying to escape.

Curses filled the air as we hesitated, the highly trained

warriors unable to fight this mighty foe.

The wind gusted back towards us and a lungful of acrid smoke choked me. Eyes streaming, I looked up to see the fire was spreading rapidly, the heat torching the trees one after the other. It was terrifying. I'd never seen such a conflagration, the closest thing I could imagine was bonfire night back home where as children my friends and I had dared one another to stand as close to the burning stack of pallets and scrap wood as we could, scorching the skin of our cheeks in the process. Already I could feel the heat and the smoke billowed back towards us, smothering us all. I could hear coughing next to me and I frantically reached out to find the closest figure, relieved when I found Rubold's form.

"Boats!" he coughed and I nodded, turning towards them but the smoke was obscuring them and in a brief burst of clear air I could see Solly staggering away, coughing appallingly as Doug ran out to drag him away from the acrid air.

It was apparent that the river was not our escape route. The boats were hidden in the smoke and I could only make out a few of my fellow humans. Rubold was hesitating beside me, looking for the rest of his team but Jacobs erupted out the smoke with Gibbo hanging off his shoulder. The Lieutenant's eyes streamed but his face was set as he saw us standing watching.

"The caves!" he snarled and Rubold mirrored his leader, hooking my arm over his shoulder and beginning to haul me mercilessly towards the canyon edge.

The caves were six feet high, low enough for me to have peered into their depths but with my leg in its splint there was no chance of me climbing. Smoke billowed again and blew between us. Rubold swore, redoubling his efforts as a voice behind me called something unintelligible.

Peeeee-hoooo

Could the source of the noise, be it human or animal follow us into the smoke? Surely not, but then what else had it done that was possible?

Peeeee-hoooo

140

"Come on!" like a rugged battering ram, Solly blew past us at a dead sprint heading for the caves. Colin and Doug followed, both running to help Jacobs with Gibbo's bulk as they caught sight of him. Of the other SEALs I could see no sign but shouting American voices sounded close at hand and I guessed they were near.

The rock face was cold and uninviting but the smoke meant I was coughing with every breath now. I hesitated as Rubold flung himself at the ledge, feet scrabbling for purchase and then he managed to climb and he was up, immediately spinning around to reach down for me. I grabbed his wrists and he pulled. My broken leg slammed into the rock face and I shouted in pain but scrabbled for purchase with my good limb. Someone grabbed me from below and shoved me, hard. I cleared the lip of the cave, spinning around as fast as I could to reach down to help but a SEAL took a running jump, landing with a grunt of effort and he was up next to me, pushing me backwards into the cave which was barely tall enough to crouch.

That suited me, I could either crawl or stand and this left me only one option. I turned into the dark, slinging my rifle awkwardly and drawing the borrowed pistol.

Dark.

Shouts from behind me and someone bawled at me to get moving. I inched forward on my belly, every movement agony as the uneven ground moved my broken leg. Whimpers of pain came unbidden from my lips as I heard shouts and coughs. The smoke had followed us in and I wondered for a mad second if we'd only climbed into our tomb but the cave opened up before me and I could smell clean air.

A beam of light stabbed the darkness and Solly pushed past me, dropping to a crouch to move through.

"Put that away!" he snapped, eyeing the pistol and I hastily holstered it, glad to have the extra hand to move myself along. Solly moved ahead as behind me voices called at me to move my carcass.

I pulled with my hands, kicked with my good leg and burned

with agony.

"Here..." Solly had reached a wider space that led upwards. He grabbed me under my arms and hauled me a good ten feet up the passage, leaving me with the torch and hastening back to help Gibbo who was groaning in agony.

I shone the light around, seeing that we were in a long, low passage perhaps four feet in height and the same in width. Water had run down here at some point because the slope I now lay on was smooth and worn. I was on my back and so I leaned my head all the way back, shining the torch further up the passage which stretched into the distance until a sharp turn which obscured my vision.

"Oi!" Solly's indignant tones reminded me I was the sole source of light and I whipped the beam back to see Colin helping him move Gibbo towards me. The ex-PSI was shivering and blood had flecked his lips. I wondered that he was still alive.

"Up here!" Jacobs' sharp American accent cut through the cave and I saw the SEALs cramming in, two of them pushing past me to face their rifles up the passage, the beams from their weapon mounted lights penetrating the darkness.

"Sound off!" Jacobs ordered and the SEALs reported in, confirming that they'd all made it.

We were all here too, what remained of us although how much longer Gibbo would last, I couldn't say. Solly caught my eye and looked significantly at my broken leg. I shrugged. There was little I could do and I secretly thanked my lucky stars that Gibbo was wounded too. Surely Solly wouldn't abandon one of his own?

Then again, if Gibbo died that would leave me as the weakest man and I suddenly began to wish that the bastard wouldn't die.

"Water?" croaked the SEAL closest to me and I reached for my canteen, grateful for the army training that had reminded me of the value the liquid brought. Every time I'd drunk over the past few days I'd refilled the metal canister from the fresh river water and the SEAL smacked his lips in appreciation, washing the taste of ash and fire from his lips.

"We need to move." Jacobs stated the obvious, looking down at Gibbo "The smoke will only get worse so we need to get out of here."

"We're not going back in a hurry." Doug pointed out.

Every man turned to look up the narrow passage. I grimaced at the thought of dragging my injured leg and Doug was looking with concern at Gibbo.

"Might kill him." he told Solly who nodded, then shrugged.

"Staying here definitely will. Dose them up and let's get moving."

Another fentanyl lozenge, this one I snatched greedily from his hand, relishing the soporific effects. Almost immediately it seemed the pain in my leg faded to a dull ache and I stared up the tunnel with renewed vigour.

"Alright, STAB." Doug gripped my shoulder "I'll help you. What's the best way you reckon?"

We began to move as Solly, Colin and two of the SEALs grabbed Gibbo and began to walk, bent almost double. The pace was painfully slow and plainly we could not keep it up for long. I tried to drag my leg along behind me but it was agony, despite the fentanyl's warm embrace. Then I began resting heavily on Doug, hopping awkwardly forward but that was excruciating.

Finally, he had to flip me over, grab me beneath the arms and drag me as I kicked with my good leg.

It was like being tortured. I tried to keep my mouth shut but grunts and whimpers of pain escaped my lips. I thanked my luck that the stone had been worn smooth by whatever water had passed this way but still it was a far cry from the smooth tarmac of a London street.

We had to stop. Gibbo was heavy and the soldiers carrying him were sweating badly. I was sweating too and Doug was panting 'hanging out' in army slang.

"Tunnel keeps going?" someone from the back called and the SEALs at the front shouted back that they couldn't see the end.

"Can you see daylight?" Jacobs called but there was no such luck.

"Alright." Solly called up "You two up there, go on ahead for a couple of minutes and let us know whats there."

"Take this!" Jacobs called and passed out a thin reel of paracord. I saw him shrug as Solly raised his eyebrows "Useful stuff to have on you."

The two men hurried off, moving up the cave and vanishing around a corner. Soon there was darkness above and below and I drew the pistol again, the solid weight a comfort in my hand.

Muttered conversations. Gibbo seemed to be delirious, murmuring gibberish in his semi-conscious state.

But there were no more whistles.

"Maybe the fire got those a-holes?" Rubold wandered out loud and there were murmurs of assent.

"At least if they come in here we can see them coming." someone reasoned. I had to agree. There were two ways in, one blocked by smoke and the other covered by the beams of our lights. Nothing was sneaking up on us here.

The cord the two SEALs had laid behind gave a twitch and then a yank and then we heard the sound of someone hurrying down the passage. Weapons were trained, I went flat on my belly raising the pistol as my heart thumped painfully.

One of the SEALs, the same one who'd swigged from my canteen came into view, shielding his eyes against the lights.

"Up here! Jacobs, you'd better come look!"

We hurried, everyone's energy restored by natural human curiosity. Doug dragged me and I kicked myself along faster than ever. We turned a sharp corner, moving out of the torchlight for a second but it didn't matter because we emerged only a minute later into a wide open cavern, the walls smooth and shining with moisture and the ceiling stretching high out of sight. A vast cave. A natural building.

Crammed with people.

I stared as the torchlight illuminated off the dozens of native men, women, and children. All of them as surprised to see us as we were them.

CHAPTER 22

There were no shouts, no gasps. Everyone just stared. I saw the fear on their faces, the injuries some of them sported. Children clung to adults, some with silent tears streaking down their faces. Something terrible had happened to these people but the longer I stared the more I saw my own expression reflected in their eyes. They looked the same as we did.

Terrified.

It didn't help when Jacobs began to snarl at them.

"Goddamn natives! Not so tough now, are ya? Who is it? Who's doing that damn whistling? Huh?"

A older woman, her faced wrinkled and weathered stood up slowly, her eyes fixed on Jacobs. Although she was unarmed and was outweighed by the Lieutenant by at least her own mass again, she did not flinch. In stark contrast to the frightened people around her she looked furious.

"You dare to come in here with your guns and your death and lecture us? You think we killed your men? Look at us! We are peaceful people! You brought death into this valley! Now you desecrate this sacred space – you!" the woman spat at Jacob's feet.

Silence filled the chamber. Jacobs looked uncomfortable. Behind the woman, the expressions of fear were increasing and I could hear a young child crying although the sobs were muffled by the mother who was rocking the infant back and forth. Disgust filled me at the fear that was rampant. I stepped forward, leaning heavily on the one crutch I'd managed to bring with me and pushed Jacobs aside, holding out my hand.

"Madam, my name is Liam. It's a pleasure to meet you."

She shook my hand. Her palm was calloused and rough.

"We came here looking for Gold and –"

"No you didn't." she whipped her hand back and snarled the words at me "You came here for –"

"Alright!" Solly snapped "No need to go into details." He stepped forward "Liam came here for Gold. We came with him."

The native woman regarded him with sympathy "I know what you came for, soldier-man. You think you're the first to come to this valley? You all knew the legends of the Nahanni."

"I came here for Gold." I spoke across Solly "What do you think he came here for?"

She regarded me coolly for a moment before speaking "This valley is ancient and the caves stretch for hundreds of miles. But did you know the river is older than the valley? Before there were mountains here the river still ran and the land rose up around it but the waters of the Nahanni cut their way through, refusing to yield their secret. Millions of years this river has flowed. You've found some of the secrets, the Gold that floats on the current but the river runs deep and there is more than Gold that hides in the depths."

I could almost feel Jacobs scoffing behind me and I hastened to keep the peace.

"Look, it's all very cryptic but we've lost a lot of men and now probably all our gear. We need to get out of here or make contact with Fort Simpson. Can you help us?"

The woman – I still didn't know her name – gave a humourless guffaw that echoed off the rock around us "Does it look like we can help you? You think we chose to shelter in these caves? You say you've lost friends but we've lost more!" she stepped forward and jabbed a finger in my chest "Before you came here this valley was a peaceful place! We lived in harmony with the – with the *river* and there was a balance. But now you had to come, you and all the others with your guns and your bombs and you didn't just turn and flee when they warned you!"

"What are they?" if my voice was raised, I thought it excusable.

146

"We don't talk about them." a male voice spoke from behind her and we all looked to see Niimi, the man who'd joined our boats upriver. His face in the torchlight looked haggard and worn and I noticed he no longer carried the hunting rifle.

"You bastard!" Solly stepped forward and grabbed Niimi's jacket but the native simply stood still and after a moment of tension. Solly let the man go.

"Why did you come with us?" I demanded.

Niimi's voice was empty of expression "To watch you. To make sure you were doing no harm. These are our lands and we have to live in harmony."

"Why did you vanish?"

"We left to come home. We had to warn our people."

"You couldn't have warned us?"

For the first time an expression of incredulity came over Niimi's face "Would you have listened? You came for Gold. What would the warnings of some ignorant native have achieved?"

"Alright, cut the crap!" Jacobs stepped forward again "I wanna know exactly what these things are that live out there in the valley! Animals? Psycho loners? And what's all that whistling about?"

"Yes." Niimi nodded.

"The fuck d'you mean 'yes'?" Jacobs shouted "What are they?"

Silence. The natives were implacable.

"They don't know." Solly murmured, transfixed by Niimi "Right? Something lives here, its what gave the valley its name but you've never seen it or given it a name."

"We avoid the valley." Niimi looked wary "Sometimes we travel past but we always keep our distance. People can travel through here and they do but some have always fallen prey to the valley." He turned to Solly "No, we don't know exactly, not in the way that you mean anyway. We don't need to. We've seen the white figures in the woods, heard the whistling and found the bodies."

"What about the missing tribe?" I suddenly remembered "The Naha?"

A hiss ran through the frightened people. Now they looked angry.

"We don't use that word." The woman snapped at me "Those people were violent and evil. They thought they could rule the valley and the valley showed them the truth of the matter. We don't use that word." she repeated.

Gibbo gave an awful, drawn out groan and at once the scene changed. The woman hurried over to his side where Doug was crouching to examine him. In a moment, a cluster of the natives were gathered around, laying him on a makeshift bed of woven cloth and examining his injuries.

"What happened?" the woman looked at me.

"Shot." I muttered "We thought by you." I looked accusingly at Niimi.

He was wide eyed "Me? Why would I shoot him?"

"There was another team." I explained "Some other group that came here too. They attacked us."

Niimi frowned "Another group of soldiers?"

"Yes."

Understanding dawned on his face "I thought they were part of your team, that you'd deceived us saying you'd all come on the river."

I stared "You saw them? Do you know where they are?"

His eyes glazed over "Dead. We found their bodies."

For some reason, this hit me hard. Despite the death, fear and agony of the past few days it was the face of the unknown sniper, riddled with bullets that filled my mind. Who had he been? Had he been the last of his team, hunted by the whistling in the woods? Had he blamed us and knowing he'd never survive lain in wait, taking his opportunity to pick us off one by one the way his friends had died? How stupid that we had fought and killed one another when we could have worked together! The waste of life was appalling and I found myself shaking my head. My leg was hurting abominably despite the fentanyl and I found a space to sit. Niimi sat next to me as the soldiers began to move into the space, setting guards at the entry and exit routes.

"What happened to Bill?" I asked Niimi and he stared at me for a few seconds before looking away. I swallowed, understanding and tried not to think of what Bill looked like without a head.

"I'm sorry that we deceived you." he muttered "I know this isn't what you wanted."

I shrugged "It's what I got." A thought occurred to me and I asked "We saw Bineshii. The man who didn't come with us on the boats?"

"I know who Bineshii is." Niimi's face turned dark.

"He stood a the top of the cliff and stared at us. What was that?"

Niimi sighed "He thought to scare you. Once we'd realised what was happening he hoped intimidation would frighten you off and the valley would be peaceful again. I told him it was stupid."

"He's dead?" I asked.

"He never came back that night."

Another headless corpse. It was a mark of how stretched my mind had become that this barely shocked me.

Rubold came and sat next to us along with another of the older SEALs, a bearded veteran named Hernandez.

"You know -" Hernandez had turned out the contents of his pack and was sharing round a big bag of dried nuts which Niimi scooped up with relish "- I heard a lot of rumours about other animals like this."

"That ate people's heads?" Rubold asked, his eyes wide.

"Nah." Hernandez shook his own head "I mean like *ancient* stuff that survived in little pockets in the wilderness. Think about it, the river has been the same habitat for like, *millions* of years."

"It must have changed though." I argued, glad of the distraction from the fear and uncertainty "The water will have changed. Different – I dunno – oxygen levels, different types of rocks leaking different sediments."

"Right but it's still water. Two hydrogen atoms, one oxygen. Water is water is water."

"Fair enough." I conceded.

"So, what if something evolved here that predates humans? Predates the valley? Over the years it just adapted every time the landscape changed. Think about it, the caves and rocks take thousands if not millions of years to be created. That's plenty of time for something to establish itself."

I knew he was trying to rationalise the enemy we faced but I couldn't help playing devil's advocate "Then how has it never been discovered?"

Rubold interjected "There was this fish a few years back or maybe a few decades that they thought was extinct but then a dude catches one somewhere and they discover there's a whole population of them. They weren't hiding really either. They were pretty much in plain sight it just took people believing they were there to go looking."

"But these aren't extinct, they're undiscovered." I pointed out.

"It's like bigfoot." Hernandez shrugged "Plenty of people up in the north of the US say they've seen sasquatch in the woods. No-one's ever found convincing evidence though. Doesn't mean they aren't there."

A piece of science from the endless content I'd consumed online after getting back to London floated to the top of my brain and I leaned back as I tried to recall it "Isn't there... something like to sustain a breeding population you need about three thousand of the species?"

Hernandez scowled at me "Maybe they don't follow normal rules? They ain't exactly behaving normally as it is."

Rubold shook his head "Nah, if they're alive then biology affects them the same as it does us. Liam's right, I remember that three thousand thing."

Hernandez scoffed another handful of nuts thoughtfully "Hey, Niimi. How many of them are there?"

Niimi turned his head away, shaking it "We shouldn't talk about them."

"Why?" the grizzled SEAL cocked an eyebrow "You think we can make our luck any worse than it already is?"

He had a point and Niimi turned back looking uncomfortable "I don't know how many there are. I don't even know *what* they are." He looked scared "I used to live in Toronto, you know. I had a normal job. We chose to come live out here like our ancestors. I don't believe in any of this stuff any more than you do." I thought he might be on the verge of tears.

"Well, it believes in you, pal, so buckle up!" Hernandez's voice was distinctly lacking in empathy "Say there are less than three thousand, they've been here a long time so maybe they live a lot longer than we do? Like, the population is declining and they're almost extinct but there's still a few hundred."

"But only trees and stuff live that long." Rubold was frowning.

Another fact, my useless brain spitting information out "Nah, there was a shark they found that was four or five hundred years old. Can't remember which."

Rubold's eyes were wide "Goddamn!" he shook his head in wonderment "Well, sharks go biting people in half every other day so if they live that long then there's no reason these suckers can't too!"

"But sharks tear people apart." I pointed out "They're predators and they use their teeth. These things cut the head off so cleanly it looked like a guillotine." I recalled Andy's words, again feeling nothing at his death. I shivered, wondering what was happening inside my head that made me so ambivalent.

"Hey, you ever seen an alligator snapping turtle?" Rubold suddenly piped up "I saw the jaws on one of them once, like a damn hydraulic press. What if this thing is some type of reptile? Big armoured hide so bullets don't do much harm, great big jaw for chompin' and don't need to eat that often so lives a long time."

I'd seen one of those on a nature documentary and I thought of the crushing press of the jaw. Rubold was right, it certainly made our enemy more believable and brought it from the realm of supernatural firmly back to nature.

But it didn't help with the fear one bit.

CHAPTER 23

Hours passed and I realised it must be night outside. The cluster of figures around Gibbo had dwindled to a pair who kept a close eye on him. The man was sedated, rapidly burning through the meagre supply of painkillers and I stared reproachfully at my injured leg as though it were to blame. Niimi seemed more comfortable sat next to me that with his own people and after a short time I saw that he was asleep. It seemed as good a use of time as any and so I leaned back against the cold rock behind me and closed my eyes.

Sleep eluded me. I was hungry but aside from Hernandez and his bag of nuts no-one else was eating. I wondered if any of us had managed to grab food from the camp or whether the flames would now have destroyed that too. Or perhaps the soldiers didn't want the natives to see their food. More mouths to feed.

I began to get caught up in a daydream about the more preferable death. The headless corpses I recalled had been otherwise unmarked. That suggested a swift ending to their pain and in the face of imminent starvation that seemed better.

"Hungry?" Niimi had been disturbed by my fidgeting. He stretched "Me too."

I sighed "You don't have any food?"

"Some." He looked away from me "We abandoned our camp when we came down here."

"Why are you down here?" I wondered.

He raised an eyebrow "To shelter."

"But why were you in the area?"

"Oh. There's a ceremony we perform. We had to pass by the

valley to get to the place where its done. When we saw you on the river we were scouting it out before the rest of the tribe made their way down."

"You said these caves were sacred?"

He looked sharply at me as if expecting a jibe but I'd been serious "There are thousands of these caves. They mostly link together and lead up and down the cliff faces. Tourists don't know about them but our people have always."

"Why?"

"Because if you say something is sacred, it keeps people away from it."

I started "You think this is where the whistling creatures live?"

A shrewd look "Where else?"

"I thought the river..."

"Did they hunt you in the water? They're in the woods, aren't they? How many predatory fish can hunt in the woods?"

I looked over my shoulder at the tunnel entrance we'd emerged from, a shiver running down my spine but Niimi shook his head.

"They aren't in here. There are thousands of caves, they aren't in every single one."

"If you knew they lived in the caves then why did you come in?"

"No-where else to run. They'd killed a whole lot of us already and at least here we can barricade the entrance."

"And starve to death."

"Shh!" he gestured at the sleeping children "Let's keep that to ourselves, right?"

I nodded apologetically "Seriously though. What are we going to do next?"

"You've got those boats..."

I told him about the fire and he shook his head in dismay.

"Anyway, we couldn't get everyone on them."

"No. And now there's no trees we can use for rafts by the sound of it."

A depressing silence.

"Well –" Niimi had false enthusiasm in his voice "I suppose we'll just have to walk!"

I stared at my broken leg and he wisely said nothing more.

With a thump and a grunt, Rubold sat down next to me, continuing our earlier conversation as though no time had passed "You know, I heard this story about some Special Forces guys that got attacked by an ogre in Afghanistan –"

"You talkin' 'bout the Kandahar Giant?" Hernandez interrupted, drawing up his previous position on the floor "Yeah – I heard that was total crap. Some dude tripped and shot himself on patrol so they made up a story to cover it up."

"Tell me." I urged.

"Well, reason I thought of it was that we were talking about animals and ancient creatures that survived." Rubold went on "But yeah, I think it was Green Berets or maybe Army Rangers were on patrol in Kandahar and they get pinged by this twelve foot monster who chucks a spear right through some poor sucker's chest. The other guys light it up and that's the end of it. The government flew it off to a black site to study it, I heard."

I frowned "I've never heard rumours of giants in Afghanistan."

"Total bullcrap, that's why." Hernandez grinned as though this were a personal victory "But now you got me thinking I remember one of the really serious bigfoot sightings."

In another life, when I wasn't sat in a cave in the Canadian wilderness surrounded by death and effectively disabled, I'd have laughed, scoffed, or left the room in disgust. But with the fear in the cave so palpable I could almost cut it and eat it, I gestured for Hernandez to continue.

"So, it was these four dudes who went hunting together every year. You know the type, seriously rugged guys, know the outdoors like the backs of their hands. So they have this cabin they built to sleep in whilst they're out hunting and one night they hear this weird whistling sound out in the darkness."

Hernandez smiled at the effect he was having. I felt a shiver run down my spine. In front of me a woman stood up with a toddler over her shoulder. The child was awake although a brightly coloured blanket wrapped around it showed the mother's futile attempt at getting it to sleep. It's eyes were big and round and locked on me as the woman headed for the back of the cave where a downwards sloping tunnel served as a latrine.

"Anyway –" Hernandez continued "- they need water and the cabin is set pretty close to this mountain spring so two of the guys, with their rifles go out to fill their canteens and they hear the whistling. One of them sees something moving towards them and thinks it's a bear so he gets it in his sights and lets a few rounds go, hoping to scare it away. Nothing happens. Then his buddy grabs him and tells him 'That ain't a bear'. The first dude asks him how he can tell because the animal is pretty far away still and the friend says, 'because it's running on two legs.'" Hernandez seemed completely oblivious to the situation we found ourselves in, instead seeming to relish his role as storyteller "So they go back to the cabin pretty damn fast and bolt the door and the other two start giving them the third degree about them not having any water but then something slams into the side of the cabin. They think it's a bear but the others tell them how the animal was on two legs. Then they heard the whistling."

Did Hernandez actually waggle his eyebrows?

"All that night they hear these creatures running around the cabin and whistling to each other, throwing rocks at the wooden walls and trying to break in. The hunters are terrified and try to shoot through small gaps in the slats but they can't get a clear shot. By the time morning comes they're all still awake and the noises outside seem to have stopped. One of them goes to the door, reasoning they need to see whats what but as he does, he sees a huge hand covering the gap that held the lock. So, he shoots it and next second they hear what sounds like a stampede as the creatures run off into the forest."

I stared at him "I think I preferred the giant story."

Rubold was scoffing "There's no bigfoot, man. Besides, who ever heard of bigfoot eating someone's head?"

"Who ever heard of anyone's head getting eaten?"

"A whole load of idiots who came here looking for Gold." I muttered and to my surprise, the two SEALs cracked up at that, shaking with laughter. I stared. Presumably the humour was lost in translation between American and English. Bloody colonials.

"Hey! Secure that!" Jacob's voice brought the mirth to an abrupt halt and we all looked around in surprise to see the native woman who had greeted us standing with a wild expression on her face. Now that I looked, the rest of the refugees were stirring, looking around and asking what was happening.

A shout and the sound of sobbing.

"What's going on?" Solly's voice was like iron as he gripped the woman's hand and I felt Niimi move beside me to stand with her. In response, she pointed to the sobbing young woman who was cowering on the floor, clutching a woven blanket to her chest.

I frowned, staring at it and trying to work out what was wrong with the picture. Suddenly the image of the wide eyed child over it's mothers shoulder filled my mind and I gasped, shaking my head in disbelief.

"Where? Where is she?" the mother looked up, shrieking at us "Where is my baby?"

Pandemonium. The natives began shouting, the mother was all but pinned down by Niimi who tried to get the story from her. Jacobs was rounding his men up, a mutinous expression on his face and was demanding to know the quickest route out of the caves.

"Liam, you need to stay here with them." Solly had gathered the remnants of his party and was leading them towards a tunnel on the far side of the cavern.

"Not a bloody chance." I grated "Drag me again if you have to but I'm not staying here to get picked off one by one."

He protested but Doug grabbed me by the shoulder and lead me over to the small tunnel where Jacobs was already preparing to move.

"How do you know it went that way?" I demanded and Jacobs snarled at me.

"Does the mother know where the kid went?"

She didn't. She'd waited for the child to relieve itself and then gone to do the same, leaving the child at the back of the main chamber. When she returned, the kid was gone.

"This was guarded though, right?" I asked.

I thought Jacobs might shoot me "Doesn't seem that way. Maybe you could've been doing that whilst you were swapping ghost stories?"

I hesitated before retorting that it had been his men who were telling the stories but it didn't seem like Jacobs cared. Instead, he was moving out, searching for the creatures.

Up, up, up we went until the stench of smoke filled the air. I wondered for a frightening moment if the entire region had been overcome by the forest fire and all we'd emerge into was the smoke and heat. On the flipside, that might mean the whistling creatures were gone or it might mean they'd been driven underground...

The cave widened and I could limp with my crutch, holding the wall with one hand. Doug stayed by me, ready to help as I wondered what on earth I was doing. I couldn't walk, could hardly shoot with one hand and the warriors that surrounded me were actively searching for the enemy. I was sure to be a headless corpse in no time but I bared my teeth in fury at my own fear, absolutely done with sitting around waiting to die. As the entrance to the cave loomed ahead, I told myself that if I was going to die, I'd go out fighting.

Maybe Valhalla was real, after all.

We erupted into air that stank of smoke but was breathable. It was dark although a bright moon shone over head. With a snap and a whooshing sound, a flare shot into the air over our heads and hung suspended by a parachute, penetrating the gloom with a ruddy glow.

"Contact left!" gunfire erupted almost immediately and I lurched away from the open ground I'd been staring into. My leg burned appallingly and I swore, reaching for the borrowed pistol.

Peeeee-hoooo

They were back. I saw a shape this time, distinctly humanoid. Was it a person?

Peeeee-hoooo

BOOM

"I got one!" Rubold was screaming his victory, the grenade launcher already primed to fire again. I stared into the glow cast by the flare seeing a huddled mass at the very furthest reach of the light. An animal? Was that black fur or was it just the shadow the dead thing sat in?

Peeeee-hoooo

Peeeee-hoooo

Peeeee-hoooo

Everywhere.

From every direction came the piercing whistles. Somehow, they seemed filled with menace and promise as though the meaning had changed to anger.

Peeeee-hoooo

Peeeee-hoooo

Peeeee-BOOM

A shrieking, terrible cry and I felt hot liquid on my face.

"Man down!" an American voice roared and I felt a thump behind me, turning to see a SEAL who's name I didn't know choking as the red ruin of his throat spelled death. Doug was there in an instant, crouching beside the man but even as he reached for the wound, the SEAL gave a gasp and went still. Doug looked up baring his teeth.

"They didn't get his head!" the dour Scot bellowed and I stared in confusion, flabbergasted that he would think of such a thing whilst crouched over the dead body.

"Back!" Jacobs was shouting, pulling us into a tighter formation. I wondered where Solly was but the stocky SAS officer appeared a moment later, running back from the edge of the flare light with gore spattering the side of his face.

"Can anyone see the kid?" that was Hernandez. At his age, I realised, he probably had children of his own and I had to admit that I'd forgotten completely about the missing child in the ambush,

Peeeee-hoooo

"Fuck you, sasquatch!" Rubold suddenly roared, flicking his weapon to full auto and standing to empty the magazine into the shadows.

Peeeee-hoooo

"That target just took half a mag of five-five-six to the chest!" he shouted, the fear in his voice almost overwhelming.

"Shut the fuck up and shoot!" Jacobs roared, furiously.

"They aren't coming into the light!" someone else shouted and as we realised this was true, the shooting ceased.

There was stillness for a moment. It was a testament to the skill and training of the operators that they were already filling empty magazines and distributing ammo. I looked around. Aside from Solly, no-one else seemed hurt and he caught my eye, looking warily at me.

"Who's down?" Jacobs elbowed me aside and knelt beside the SEAL "Shit, they got Mitchell!" he shouted and I heard a mixture of curses, a shout of pain and an oath of revenge forming a vicious chorus.

"He was shot..." Doug suddenly pointed out and Jacobs dropped to the ground, peering closely at Mitchell's torn throat.

"Goddamn!" he swore "The other team must still be out there!" the dead face of the anonymous sniper filled my mind.

We were stuck. The light kept the creatures back but it silhouetted us against the rock we'd emerged from. None of us had heard the shot but the sound of our own gunfire had been deafening. I stared at the pistol in my own hand realising I'd done nothing but stand and stare.

"I'm going to check that kill, Sir!" Rubold suddenly announced and Jacobs shouted at everyone to cover him as the young SEAL, apparently unafraid hastened across to the thing he'd shot. I stared, leaning forward to see what it was, desperate to finally understand some answers about what had brought us here.

"What you got?" Hernandez sounded as cool as ever.

Crack

This time we all heard the shot. Rubold went down hard but was moving already, scrabbling back in a frantic crawl towards the shelter of our barrels.

"Goddamn, back inside!" Jacobs roared and we moved back into the cave, stopping a few metres short of the entrance. I tried to drop next to Rubold but lost my balance and instead fell next to him. The young SEAL was grimacing in pain.

"Where're you hurt?" I demanded and he indicated his leg.

"Hey, fellas!" he called in a shaky voice "I got shot in both legs! Do I get a prize?"

"No, mate." Doug crouched beside him, examining the wound "But if you get a third, the President has to give you a lap dance."

"Where does the third wound have to be?"

"Ah, that's the bad news..." Doug cut Rubold's trousers open and examined the bullet "You'll be alright, pal." He began to dress the wound.

"What now?" someone asked and the silence that followed his words spoke volumes.

"Back into the cave?" I suggested, ignoring Jacobs' sharp look "What? We can't get out there without being shot."

"We're not far from where I scouted when I came up." Doug had switched off his light but I recognised Solly's voice in the dark. He was close by me and stank of some putrid odour "Maybe two hundred metres to the right is a natural little bowl in the rocks. Plenty of cover from incoming fire and the ground will stop those things coming at us so fast."

I heard Jacobs grunt in agreement and then ask Rubold if he could walk.

"All good here." Rubold made a meal out of standing though and grunted in pain "Hey, anymore of that heroin stuff?"

"No."

Jacobs made a decision "Alright, Hernandez, you help Rubold. I'll carry the limey cripple." I felt his arm wrap around me and

160

kept my mouth shut. He could insult me until we got out of here so long as he kept me alive.

"Everyone ready?" no one replied in the negative so the Lieutenant must have assumed that meant 'yes'. He gave a sharp word of command and next second I cracked my head on the roof of the cave, ducking to avoid any further impacts and allowing Jacobs to haul me along the rocky ground.

Out into the open, stumbling and slipping my leg burning like fire. I kept my mouth shut, biting down on the pain and concentrating on moving as fast as I could.

Movement to my left, surely there were none of our guys there? I reached for the pistol that I'd holstered and Jacobs began to protest then he suddenly flung me to the ground and a white beam of light stabbed the darkness and I saw the light reflected off his teeth as the SEAL fired round after round into the darkness and roared his battle fury.

A vague rushing sound, a roar of pain and the sound of a knife being drawn in a hurry then the light went spinning away and I turned over, whipping the unfamiliar pistol from its holster.

"Shoot it!" Jacobs' voice had finally lost it's anger and was now filled with panic. Ahead I could hear American voices shouting and light stabbed the gloom, searching where we lay but missing us.

Two dark figures illuminated by the moonlight, one distinctly human by the shape of its helmeted head –"

Bang-bang-bang-bang

The pistol jerked in my hands, the rounds erupting from the end of the barrel and something gave a scream of pain and Jacobs hit the ground next to me with a curse.

"Come on!" I shouted and tried to stand but my crutch was gone, lost in the dark and so I crawled, driving my one good leg forward and dragging the SEAL with me.

"Sir!" Hernandez had come back and he tripped over me before grabbing us both and running backwards, one man gripped in each hand, an incredible feat of strength "Friendly incoming!" he shouted through gasping breaths and then we were bumping over rough stones and I could hear familiar voices and I knew we'd reached the shelter of Solly's sanctuary.

"Sir?" someone was shaking Jacobs.

"I think he's knocked out." I remembered the man collapsing next to me with a grunt. At least his head was intact and a moment later I heard him come round with a groggy voice.

"He's good!" Hernandez had apparently assumed command of the SEALs and was calling orders. Solly had moved his surviving men into position without much conversation and I scrambled for the closest large boulder, calling out in a low voice that it was me.

"Alright, STAB?" it was Colin and the man seemed totally unfazed.

"Living the dream, mate."

"Aren't we all." I saw a faint gleam as he checked the time "Few more hours until daylight. We can get a brew on then, eh?"

Peeeee-hoooo

"How many hours?" I asked, deep longing in my voice.

CHAPTER 24

They came again twice more before dawn. The whistles never ceased and we heard running footsteps around us but Solly had chosen well and as the grey light of yet another dawn spread across us, I could see that the natural bowl we sat in was backed by the sheer drop into the canyon and dotted with enough boulders that every man had excellent cover. Indeed, no shots were fired and as our line of sight improved, no animals were seen either.

"Solly." I crawled over to him, seeing the deep lines of exhaustion on his face that I knew must be mirrored on my own.

"What?"

"You came here for them, didn't you?"

He looked at me as though I were mad, half his face still covered in the blood that was plainly not his own "Piss off."

"No." I moved into a sitting position next to him "You ran out of formation last night to get to one of those things, didn't you? What did you get, a blood sample?"

He glowered at me with his iron grey eyes. That might have terrified me, after all this was the man who'd seriously considered murdering me. But Solly was the least frightening thing out here.

I stared him out and finally, I saw something relent in his eyes "Alright." he lowered his voice, looking around "The SEALs are here because of an intel package they intercepted from us."

"About something that's here in the valley?"

"In the area, yeah. Those animals..." Solly's voice trailed off.

I took a breath "Do you actually know the full details?"

He stared at me again. This time there was less ice in his eyes and more sadness. I thought I understood. He'd brought his men on this mission, perhaps following orders as he was trained or perhaps because of something he'd heard that he believed was his responsibility. Either way, there was more to this than he knew and now his friends were dead, there were a whole group of civilians that needed protection and he was here being hunted by the very things he'd been sent to examine.

"What are they?"

"I don't know."

"Are they animals?"

"Could be."

"Genetic mutated freaks gone wrong?"

He grinned humourlessly "Sounds more likely than bigfoot."

I rolled my eyes. Solly wasn't telling me the full truth but perhaps he didn't know the full truth.

"What about the Gold?"

"What about it? It was a good excuse."

"And Vlad?" I remembered the old man back in the bunker in Europe "You fed him that story?"

It was Solly's turn to roll his eyes "'Course I did! He told it well though. When you came to me with the idea of coming here I jumped on it."

I didn't understand and I told him so. He looked exasperated.

"Does it matter?"

"Look, if any of us make it out of here, it's not going to be me." I didn't really believe that in my heart of hearts but I did want to know what Solly was hiding "I want to know what I'm dying for."

A big sigh "Fine. We –"

"Who's 'we'?"

"Intelligence. Special Forces. People above your pay grade, Lance-Sergeant."

I blinked "Alright."

"*We* realised the Yanks were hacking some of our communications. We told our bosses but they wanted proof."

Solly shrugged "This just so happened to be a good excuse to test that theory. We sent a message saying there was a genetic modification program here in the valley that was creating super soldiers. We made up some crap about a couple of tourists going missing and that we'd blamed it on the legends about headless bodies appearing here. Then we said an SAS team disguised as a gold hunting expedition was coming to take out the remaining test subjects. That's why I brought all this kit." He indicated the rifle and weapons we carried.

"You were going to fight the American team?" I asked incredulously.

"What? No. But if they can intercept it then so can... the enemy." he raised an eyebrow and I caught his drift.

"That's who –" I nodded towards the forest and Solly gave a grim nod of his own.

I sat back, letting out a long sigh. I expected to feel relieved that I finally knew the secret that Solly had kept from me. It seemed so utterly ridiculous that my life was being thrown away for such trivial bullshit, so pedestrian that Johannes, Jeff, Martin, Robbie, and Andy were all dead along with the SEALs and now presumably the missing natives.

"Why Gibbo?" I asked as the thought occurred to me.

"Oh. Yeah, I'm actually sorry about that." Solly grimaced "Honestly, I thought he'd just piss you off so much that you'd send us and stay back yourself. He was supposed to come ahead and help you prep back in Fort Simpson but some other stuff came up and by that time I'd briefed him so he had to come."

"Thanks for that."

"Yeah." Solly nodded "If we ever get back to the In and Out club, I'll stand you a beer."

"You'll stand me a lifetime membership and all my bar bills." I swore and despite everything, Solly laughed.

Peeeee-hoooo

And that was it, the final piece of the puzzle. I looked at Solly, seeing the resignation on the grizzled soldier's face "What about them? The creatures?"

Solly looked pained, puffing out his cheeks and letting out a long breath "Yeah. I'll be honest mate, I didn't expect that."

Peeeee-hoooo

Peeeee-hoooo

They were getting closer. I couldn't see anything but the whistles were getting louder. The tension rose as fingers tightened on triggers and eyes twitched left and right. It was broad daylight, where the hell were they?

Crack

Crack-crack-crack-crack-crack

The unmistakeable sound of massed rifle fire, this coming from the woods. To me, the noise of a section of soldiers opening fire had always sound like a dried bundle of twigs being snapped in someone's hands and the noise brought back memories of sweaty, sleep deprived training exercises in the soaking landscape of Wales.

"Hold fire!" Jacobs seemed to have recovered enough to call orders. Solly was leaning out from behind his rock, apparently heedless of the incoming gunfire but a second later, I realised there was none. The shots were coming from the forest and between them came the sounds of whistles, at least one cut short mid shriek.

BOOM

A great jet of smoke lanced up from the trees, several hundred metres away from us. I ducked instinctively but there was no danger. The massed gunfire seemed to pause for a moment as if the shooters were catching their breath and then it erupted again, this time seeming to double in ferocity and we heard distinctly human voices shouting in a frenzy.

"That's the other team." Solly told me, speaking in a normal voice to be heard over the sounds of battle.

"Who –" I started but then nodded "Someone else intercepted the intel?" the irony that in eight months of so-called 'war' this was the closest I'd come to the enemy was not lost on me.

Solly gave me a big nod then suddenly dropped flat as the unmistakeable whip of a bullet passing close by sounded.

"Are they shooting at us?" I asked but it was plain the shots were stray rounds as the battle moved. I pressed myself close to the ground, appreciating for the first time the real dangers of stray bullets.

Peeeee-hoooo

Closer again, this one out of my line of vision to my left back the way we had run in the dark from the cave entrance.

Peeeee-hoooo

"Holy mother of God!" Rubold's voice sounded. I couldn't hear him but I heard his blasphemy echoed by another American voice and then Doug's Scottish tones rising above every other voice.

"What the fook is that?"

"Enemy sighted?" I joked to Solly and he shouted for a description. I thought I understood his idea. At the very least he could provide an understanding of what these things were and then his mission might be considered a success, the deaths of his men having at least counted for something.

"Big, black and fucking fast!" Rubold was shouting a target description. I could see Doug nodding, his face pale beneath the dirt that streaked all our skin.

BOOM

A second explosion from the woods. I prayed another fire wouldn't start.

Peeeee-hoooo

The sounds were diminishing now although gunfire still sounded from the woods. It was lessening though as the unknown shooters either burned through their ammunition or were killed.

I swallowed, wondering if that was about to be the same for us.

"Movement in the trees!" it was Jacobs and I leaned out from behind my rock to see figures in the treeline, this one far thinner and less overgrown than its counterpart down in the valley.

Solly moved beside me, grabbing the binoculars that I still carried and crawling forward to the front of the line of troops. He peered at the figures which I could see were peeling backwards in a classic tactical manoeuvre.

Human, then.

"Rubold!" he snapped at the young SEAL with the injured legs "Light them up!"

I moved to the right, unslinging my rifle. From this range, I could hit them easily and I sighted on a figure that was kneeling at the treeline, using a tree for cover from whatever enemy stalked them from the woods. They'd not seen us though and the ambush was perfect.

BOOM

No time to worry about the futility of massacring each other in the face of a common enemy, no thoughts to waste feeling sorry for them, we opened fire as one. I fired once, seeing the round impact the kneeling figure and send it crashing down. More movement and I fired a second and a third as Rubold lobbed the oversized grenades into the treeline.

Slaughter.

What the beasts that stalked us had failed to do, we managed in just a few seconds. Smoke filled the air above the trees, mixing with the faint grey that still lingered from the forest fire below us. Nothing moved.

Magazines were replenished, someone passed around a bottle of water, probably the last that we had.

"No movement." Hernandez had produced a complicated looking optic and was scanning the treeline slowly, checking carefully "Nothing on thermals. Think we got them all, Sir."

Jacobs nodded, turning to the rest of his men "Thermal scope doesn't mean there aren't more! No-one breaks cover without my clearance. Remember, these things are still out here with us and they're the primary threat!"

Voices called out in the affirmative and we all went quiet, listening for the whistles that would surely signify the creatures coming to finish what they'd started.

We didn't have long to wait.

CHAPTER 25

Movement to our left and I moved to the other side of my rock to sight on the creature, desperate for a full look at our elusive enemy but instead it was Niimi, running full tilt towards us.

"Friendly!" I roared although no-one had moved to fire on the native. Sweating and wide-eyed, Niimi crashed to lie flat inside the ring of soldiers. Solly was next to him immediately, demanding to know what had caused the man to risk his life.

"They're in the caves!"

I felt sick. I saw in my mind's eye those terrified faces, the children, the old and imagined the whistling echoing off the cold rock.

"Gibbo!" Doug snapped and I remembered the injured SAS man with a guilty start, having forgotten we'd left him behind.

"Alright!" Solly looked around, searching for Jacobs "We're going back –"

"Yeah, we're comin' too!" the American snapped but no-one moved. Instead, every eye turned to the smoke rising from the forest.

The silence spoke volumes.

"If he got here, we can get there!" Doug hissed and Solly nodded, looking at me.

"You gonna make it?"

"Limey's gonna be fine!" Hernandez grabbed me by the arm and I felt butterflies in my stomach at the thought of the pain the short distance would bring. My leg throbbed.

"Alright!" Solly assumed the voice of command "Assume the enemy is still out there with weapons on us! Basic movement drills! No-one moves without their buddy covering them. We go in two sections, wounded men split between them. Prepare to move!"

Voices echoed the command and I tensed, relief flooding me when Doug grabbed my other shoulder. Between him and Hernandez, I was apparently not to be responsible for my own movement, instead grimacing as I was dragged at a dead sprint. I held my breath for the bullets that would tear from the forest or the mysterious shape that would lurch with its piercing whistle to snap heavy jaws on the soft skin of my neck, ending this nightmare once and for all but instead we stopped, dropping hard to the ground and I obediently trained by rifle on the treeline as the second group sprinted past us, Rubold limping badly.

Nothing. No whistles, no shots. Somehow, that scared me more. Where were they?

"Move!" Solly snapped and I was up again or – more accurately, Hernandez and Doug were up, hauling my useless form forward as I tried to keep the rifle steady which was impossible when being pulled by your armpits.

Peeeee-hoooo

"Fuck off!" snapped Doug and we went flat, every nerve tense. How far was it to the cave entrance? Would we miss it? It had been dark when we'd emerged and the hole wasn't large. What if we ran straight past it and were trapped out in the open? I ground my teeth swearing that if I died for Gibbo, I'd come back to haunt the HAC to punish them for inflicting him on me,

Peeeee-hoooo

"Move!" the second team had passed us, dropped flat and now we bounded past them. I saw something in the trees and shouted but we didn't check our pace.

"Move!"

Jacobs led the charge, passing us, dropping to one knee and aiming his barrel to cover his men.

Peeeee-hoooo

I thought I saw the creature that made the noise this time, a dark shape standing half behind a tree. It looked human and I narrowed my eyes but we were moving again and focussing was a struggle.

Peeeee-hoooo

Definitely there. I could see the dark shape but I couldn't see the detail. Was it hairy? Wearing clothes? How tall was it?

Peeeee-hoooo

"Just sod off!"

"Shut up!" Solly snapped and Doug went silent. I could see the Scot's lip was curling. Was he losing his cool finally?"

Peeeee-hoooo

"Screw this!" Jacobs was panting but he turned, sighted on the tree line and fired a series of short, controlled bursts.

Peeeee-hoooo

Peeeee-hoooo

Peeeee-hoooo

A chorus of the whistles rose and now we could all see the shapes moving around, keeping behind the trees. Dumb animals? I didn't think so. I aimed through the rifle sights but they used the trees for cover, twisting behind the trunks. What kind of animal did that?

"There!" every eye looked to see Niimi pointing to the mouth of the cave. Relief washed over me for a second but then I remembered the darkness, the terrible pitch blackness and imagined the whistling sounds echoing from the rocks.

Peeeee-hoooo

Then again, it was almost literally a choice between a rock and a hard place. For some reason I laughed at that, a short, high pitched giggle that made me more scared than anything. Even if I got out of this, I'd never sleep another night through, never be able to hear a whistle without my guts churning. Was it even worth it?

Peeeee-hoooo

Suddenly getting into the caves seemed very worth it and we were moving, barrels of rifles covering us from front and rear and then we all saw the moment where a creature broke forth from the tree line and began to move.

Fast.

So fast.

A strong jaw.

Ivory teeth.

Hair.

BOOM

Rubold, a grin on his face that would make the devil himself shiver launched a grenade and the monster vanished in a burst of smoke. The thump hit my face and we heard a terrible drawn out scream of agony.

"Did you see it?"

"Goddamn bigfoot!"

"Didn't look anything like sasquatch!"

"Get in the goddamn caves!"

Back into the dark, the torchlight lighting our way as the cold rock seemed to beckon.

Peeeee-hoooo

Echoing down the tunnel behind us, chasing us, herding us.

"Down here!" Niimi's voice, his flat, expressionless face suddenly visible in the torchlight and then he led us down a right turn, his heels visible as he moved fast.

Agony in my broken leg. Tears in my eyes.

Peeeee-hoooo

They were behind us. I could hear American voices yelling and then a shot, impossibly loud in the confined space.

"Got it!"

"It's still moving!"

"Move! Move!"

And then, miraculously we were back in the vast chamber where the refugees had sheltered and Niimi was stepping past us and then the light left him and when it shone back on the spot he'd occupied the man was gone…

"Son of a bitch!" Jacobs' voice was irate. Lights flashed around the room and then more voices joined him. I felt my heart in my throat and stared.

"Where'd they go?"

"Where's Gibbo?" Doug's voice was furious now. The Scot roared into the darkness "Gibbo!"

"Shut up!" Solly was back "Where's Niimi?"

"Goddamn vanished!"

"There's a tunnel..."

A small crevice between two rocks. We all stared, seeing how you'd have to stand from a certain angle and shine the torch directly at it to see it. Or, you'd have to know it was there.

"This isn't right." Hernandez still didn't sound scared but he was as close as I thought he'd ever get to losing his trademark cool.

"Is there anything around here?" someone was trying to make sense of the empty chamber, trying to logicise the nightmare we couldn't wake up from.

"Nothing. They took everything."

"It's a trap." Solly's voice was cold and devoid of feeling "If they'd run, they'd have left gear behind. And someone moved Gibbo."

As if in response, a very male yell of pain sounded from down a tunnel.

"Was that him?"

"Could have been..."

Peeeee-hoooo

A second scream. Doug ran across the chamber, stopping as his torch illuminated at small opening "Gibbo!"

Peeeee-hoooo

"They're down here!"

Everyone moved across. This was the tunnel that had been used as a latrine and the stench was appalling. A filthy mass of waste coated the rock as Doug covered his nose with a gloved hand.

Peeeee-hoooo

Faint but audible. How far had they dragged the injured man?

"Let's go!" Solly led the way. Doug dragged me and I tried not to think of the terrible substance I was being hauled through.

Bile rose in my throat and if I'd had anything in my stomach it would've come back up. I heard a SEAL gagging.

Peeeee-hoooo

Louder now. My palms began to sweat. I'd slung the rifle across my shoulder and now drew the pistol, trying my best to stagger along with Doug.

Peeeee-hoooo

Up ahead? I tried to look but cracked my head on the rock. I had to concentrate on moving but I thought I saw something dark moving between the beams of torchlight.

"Engaging!"

BOOM-BOOM-BOOM-BOOM

For a second I thought Rubold had fired his grenade launcher, a surely suicidal action in this cold tomb of a cave but instead it was gunfire, the sound amplified a million times and I cried out, clamping my hands over my ears as my head rang with the shock.

"Cease firing!"

"Doug!"

I was dropped unceremoniously and I collapsed on the floor, fortunately now clear of the sewage that lay behind us. I rolled onto my front, trying to see what had taken our medic and I froze, my head trying to rationalise the horror my eyes were seeing.

Gibbo, his upper body naked and dark with masses of bruising was tied to a pair of iron hoops set into the rock. He hung limp from them, small moans of agony coming from his lips. Doug and Solly were already trying to release his hands, frantically searching their kit for tools. I looked at Gibbo's chest, on which was drawn a crude symbol in red –

I cringed.

The symbol had been carved into his torso with a knife, the hilt of which I could see now protruded from his belly. An ornate, wooden handle with complex patterns carved into it.

Niimi's knife.

Peeeee-hoooo

Solly froze, staring into the darkness beside him. Someone shone a light and I saw a dark blur move through the tunnels, racing to where Gibbo hung.

BOOM

The shots were so loud. I clamped my hands over my head, cringing in agony as lights flickered. A couple went out and suddenly everyone was shooting and I could just make out the whistles between shots and I tried to think through the agony, aiming the pistol but I couldn't see, couldn't think and then hot liquid splashed on me. For a crazy moment I thought I was still in the latrine and someone had mistaken this section of cave for a place to piss and I rolled out the way before recognising the blood for what it was.

The shooting was louder. I heard Solly roar in anger and in a flash of a weapon light I could see Gibbo still hung from the wall but his head was gone...

I started to crawl. My head rang like a church bell and sounds were indistinct. I tried to fight but there was no enemy I could see. A dark opening yawned before me and I dragged myself into its depths, begging for shelter. I wanted to pull the cold rock around me like a child's blanket, shutting out the death and the monsters and the terrible, awful screams of men who were surely now dying...

A tunnel, cold rock and the need to keep moving, to flee the danger. Voices faded, screams died and the boom of gunfire faded to a pop, then died and I was alone in the darkness. I knew the whistling creatures were behind me, chasing and stalking me. Why didn't they attack? I grunted with every pull, the sound strangely muted to my deafened ears and my leg throbbed. I fancied I could feel the two parts of bone rubbing together and let out a shrill giggle at the thought. Why were they fighting the soldiers? Come for me! The useless, broken, spineless STAB! I couldn't be an easier target! Somewhere, I knew, the natives were laughing at us, jubilant at the trap they'd set. I wondered what the ritual they'd come to complete really was. A human sacrifice? An appeasement to the ancient monsters they coexisted with? The giggle followed me all the way as the tunnel began to slope downwards, the realisation of it all striking me and seeming hilarious as I thought of the Naha tribe that had vanished, their rituals no doubt spoiled by some greedy member of the tribe who'd taken the tribute for themselves or perhaps a sacrificial victim who'd fought back, refusing to give their head to appease the beasts. I wondered how many of the men whose deaths had given the valley its name had come to the same realisations that I had. Had they laughed like I was in the face of speeding death? Had they shaken their heads at the futility of fighting such monsters? Or had they not seen them, never sensed the danger until it was too late and they were forever sundered from their bodies?

The tunnel was sloping downwards so steeply now that I was almost falling. I laughed at that, thinking how disappointed my pursuers would be to end the chase so dully. Me, my neck broken at the bottom of a deep hole. Or perhaps they'd never find me and my corpse would rot here, locked inside the rock as my spirit wandered the endless hallways and caves, laughing maniacally.

That scared me into sobriety. I stopped in the darkness. The thought of never leaving here where the oppressive darkness hurt my eyes and the cold rock made me shiver was more frightening than the thought of my own death. I began to fade from sheer panic back to being merely terrified. Where was I? How far had I crawled down this tunnel? I was facing downwards so steeply that I thought I'd never make it back up the slope. Should I turn around? But I couldn't, the rock was too tight and I felt a terrible sense of claustrophobia, knowing that I was trapped. My breathing rose to a sharp pant and I began to wonder if I'd run out of air.

Keep moving

Down, sliding now on the wet rock and then after a minute, or a year, I felt icy water on my hands. I stopped, or rather, I tried to stop but the slope was too steep and the rock beneath me was wet and smooth, eroded by the small stream I'd been slithering through and I lost my grip and before I could stop myself, could grip the walls of the tiny space I was trapped in, I fell face first into the water's icy embrace.

CHAPTER 26

I couldn't turn, couldn't go back and couldn't see. Breathing was impossible and my lungs began to burn immediately. Had I taken a breath before I slid in? I couldn't remember and I floundered for a moment, knowing that this was death.

Was it so bad? At least I'd die whole, my body and mind connected. That was more than could be said for Gibbo, Martin, Jeff, Robbie, Andy and Mitchell. Not to mention the other SEALs and the unknown shooters who'd died in the small stretch of woodland that had clung to the side of the raging Nahanni. I wondered briefly who they were, it seemed important to remember everyone in my final thoughts. A half second later that seemed stupid. After all, this was my death and I didn't have to share it with anyone.

My mouth opened. I didn't remember relaxing my jaw but the ice cold water flowed over my tongue making my gums throb. Liquid pooled into my ears, soothing the pain the gunfire had beaten into them. It was blissful in a way and I held onto that as I realised I had no more breath and very soon I was going to have to inhale the icy waters of the Nahanni and give myself over to its embrace. I thought of my parents, of Adam's warnings, of the announcement of my death back at the HAC. Would the Commanding Officer announce it in front of the massed soldiers? Would my name sit on the roll of honour? It was hard not to see myself as a casualty of war.

Bright white light burning into my skull. If this was dying, it was more painful than I'd hoped and I braced myself for the agony of my passing but instead rough hands were grabbing me and I instinctively allowed myself to be pulled, the habit formed from long hours of being dragged by Doug.

Air. Beautiful, clean, dry air.

Agony.

The burning pain of life. I was alive. I was out of the water. There were no words for the pain that racked every inch of my body. Bright light forced my eyes shut and a muffled voice was speaking but there was water in my ears, or perhaps it was blood?

I risked a peek at the light. A dark figure, face obscured by shadow. One of the creatures? Had they rescued me to claim my head? It seemed important not to let them have this final victory and I thrust my head back beneath the water.

"Liam!"

A voice, familiar and filled with fury. Solly? But there was an accent. Not American but softer...

"Niimi!" I gasped and felt for the pistol on my hip but the sturdy native man was pulling me out of the water, laying me on the cold stone and I realised with a jolt that he'd saved my life.

"...alright?"

That was the only word I could make out but the meaning was clear. What was more transparent though was the absolute fact that I was anything but alright. I could feel myself shivering, understanding that the cold was as much of a threat as the bullets of the foreign team or the teeth that I'd seen...

Had I seen that? Now that my mind replayed the image I was struck by the ridiculousness of the vision. Surely what I'd seen was an animal, no supernatural entity? The long teeth – what creature evolved such implements? Nothing in biology as I understood the subject lent itself to tools that were surely only developed for a single purpose.

"...with me...!" Niimi's face swam across my vision again. He pointed to my ears and I stared stupidly at him before reaching up as though in a trance to feel my left ear.

Congealed and blocked by blood. I understood and reached down to splash the icy water on the thick glob, trying not to think about where it came from. Was my brain oozing blood?

"... need to move." Niimi was saying and I stared at him. He was bleeding from the ears too, clearly how he'd understood my own condition so swiftly. A trio of deep gashes ran down the side of his face and I stared at them, seeing the fresh blood.

"How are you here?" I choked out, my voice gritty and crackling. I spat into the water, seeing bloody phlegm float in the torchlight.

"I ran..."

"From what?" my eyes landed on the scratches on his face, the three lines the perfect width apart for the hooked fingernails of a human to have scratched him.

Niimi lowered his gaze for a second, just enough for me to see the guilt in his expression. He turned, gesturing once again for us to leave.

"You set us up."

Wide eyed, he shook his head.

"Really? You're going to lie to me in here?"

Niimi just stared and I saw the fear in his eyes. I shook myself, getting out of the cave was my priority here.

"This way!"

As he shone the torch around, I saw that the passage stretched before us, leading down. Behind me, a deep pool of black water lapped against solid rock. Had the tunnel I'd slid down led me under the water? I wondered if I'd simply wriggled another foot that I might have made it through the water myself.

Maybe not.

Niimi was moving, heading off at a speed that I could not match. My leg was burning as though a hot poker had now filled the space between the two broken parts of the bone. I reached out both hands, leaning on the sides of the passageway and hopping awkwardly. A minute later and I was sweating, the shivers dying a death as certain as my own was sure to be.

"How far?" I hissed and Niimi turned back, his face white in the torchlight.

"Soon. This comes out by your boats..."

So that was where we were headed? I wondered what had happened to the rest of Niimi's people. Had he abandoned them to their fate? How had he got ahead of me? Was his cowardice the reason for the scratches on his face? My lip curled.

"There!" he pointed and I saw for the first time the faint glimmer of light. Real daylight, pouring in through a narrow fissure in the rock. It took more agonising minutes for me to shuffle my way to it. My hands were bleeding from the roughness of the rock walls. Whereas the floor was smooth and worn by water the edges were razor tipped and I wondered if the passage had been widened by tools. Not that it mattered now.

"Come on!" Niimi had reached the light but, depressingly it was simply a crack, not wide enough for us to squeeze through. I stared at the river running past, greedily absorbing the daylight.

"How much further?" Why was I asking that? It didn't matter. How ever far it was, I'd make it.

"The fire has stopped."

It was true. The air was clear although the faint whiff of ash caught my nostrils. Would the boats still be there? Surely the fire had reached our camp and obliterated all the kit along with the bodies that lay unburied on the shore.

Back into the darkness, descending all the time and more fissures appeared. I could see the forest now or rather, what remained of it. The fire had left blackened trunks standing and emptied the earth beneath of every living thing, carpeting it all in a grey layer of ash.

A boat!

I could see the edge of our camp and a single boat lay where we'd left them but the sun was shining and the way the beam fell meant I could see only a black shape. No way to tell if it would float.

"Okay." Niimi had slowed. Ahead, daylight showed through a wide opening. One of the caves we'd seen from the camp "I'll go first. The drop isn't too bad but you might need to lean on me."

"I'll make it." I growled.

"We need to get to the boats." Niimi was peering across the

light "Once we're past the hot springs, we'll be safe."

I said nothing. I stared at Niimi.

"What?"

I bared my teeth, thinking of all the dead "You led us here. This was a trap. Your 'ritual'." I layered the word with as much disgust and derision as I could muster "You brought us here to sacrifice us."

"We didn't lead anyone here. You came looking for Gold. Didn't you hear the stories?" Niimi had rediscovered his backbone and looked angry.

"Stories you started."

"The stories are far older than you or I. They're a warning. A plea to keep people away from the valley."

"Away from the creatures?"

"Yes."

"What are they."

He shrugged as though it didn't matter.

White hot anger flashed through me. I thought of all the dead that filled the canyon and were buried in the caves around us. Of Doug who'd tended me and of Rubold with his wicked sense of humour.

"How many more will you kill?" I snarled.

He bared his own teeth "None! Didn't you hear back in the caves? They tore us apart!"

A silence loaded with injustice filled the air between us. A part of me knew that he was right. Another part of me could only think of what this man represented. Decades of death, of luring innocent people to placate the monstrous beings who lived in the valley and stalked the caves. What was the point? Tradition?

"Is everyone else dead?" I asked.

"Yes."

"You're certain?"

"I'm not about to go back and check!" Niimi exclaimed.

"Good." I declared and shot him.

He'd been pointing the torch so that its light spread across the tunnel, illuminating enough for us both to see equally. In the shadows, he hadn't seen the pistol that I'd drawn from the holster. How it had remained in place was a mystery but it was a testament to the quality of the kit that Solly had brought.

The bullet punched a hole through Niimi's lying face and blew the back of his head away in a dark spray of gore. He was flung backwards, dead in an instant.

Next second, I was almost dead. The noise of the shot was like being stabbed in my already injured ears and I screamed at the pain. But darkness had filled the cave as Niimi fell on the torch and I staggered forward, pulling the light from under him and shining it on his face, feeling nothing as I saw his staring wide eyes.

I spat on his corpse and headed for the light.

*

One of the boats was mostly undamaged. The other two were smoke blackened and looked about as sailable as the Titanic. I took the only option and flung myself into it after frantically casting about for food.

There was none. Nothing but Gold and corpses lying in the ruins of a madman's dream.

The engine started, thank God, but immediately it became apparent that the hull was cracked. Water was flooding in at an alarming rate and I couldn't steer the boat and plug the leak at the same time. Memories of the small beach I'd sheltered on with Johannes came to me and I stared ahead, praying that my luck wouldn't fail me now.

Peeeee-hoooo

Faint and far away. I turned, baring my teeth and reaching for the rifle only to discover I'd lost it somewhere in the caves.

The towering walls of the canyon loomed on either side as I stared at the rising water level in my boat. The steering was becoming sluggish and my progress was only kept up by the fast current.

There!

The small beach appeared around a bend and I let out a shout of joy. At least I could happily die of starvation or exposure rather than drowning. A small mercy.

I ran the boat ashore, hard and staggered over the side, my eyes landing on a pair of black crates at the rear of the craft. I stared as the river rushed past and then I busted up, doubling over and roaring with helpless, maniacal laughter. Not the madman hysteria of the caves but a true, deep, belly laugh because Johannes, in perhaps the last act of a Gold fevered man had shoved the two meagre crates of Gold dust into this craft and it was their weight that had forced the boat to sit lower and heavier in the water and filled the hull with so much liquid that I was now trapped.

A rich man.

A dead man.

I laughed until I collapsed on the beach.

CHAPTER 27

The most ordinary thing in the world saved my life.

Tourists.

The laughter reached me first. Someone was telling a joke in a loud voice, the words echoing off the steep sides of the canyon. I could hear paddles being dipped in the rushing water by clumsy hands. Was this Solly? Had he and the survivors escaped the tunnels? Were they laughing at the slaughter they'd inflicted on the whistling monsters and now readying their weapons to finish me, the coward who'd abandoned them to their fate?

"Ahoy there!"

It seemed impossible that amidst the blood, smoke, and death someone could sound so happy, so filled with joy and hope. What was there to be so optimistic about? I lay on my side, the cold pebbles of the beach pressed uncomfortably against the side of my head. My eyes were open and staring. I couldn't remember the last time I'd blinked. For some reason that seemed important.

"Ahoy there! Are you hurt?"

Was I hurt? My leg was broken and I fancied a thousand small bruises and cuts covered my skin. My ears, although painful seemed intact and as I considered my answer to the question, I pulled a face and moved my head from side to side as if uncertain.

A sharp stabbing sensation as a jagged piece of rubble from the crumbling cliff poked into my scalp. I flinched away from it, the small movement turning into a spasm as I rolled then yelled out in agony as the bones in my leg moved together.

"Over here!"

"Quick!"

"Get the radios!"

But there was no signal here. We'd been unable to contact anyone for the past week. Wasn't that why we'd stayed in the hell hole that was the Nahanni? I could think of no other reason beyond the obstinate arrogance of men who would not know when they were beaten.

Soft hands on my arms, unfamiliar faces twisted with concern. Who was I? Where was my team? Was I hurt?

"Get back!" I snarled, reaching for the pistol but the weapon was gone. I had no idea when I'd lost it. Perhaps after I'd murdered Niimi I'd dropped it? I didn't remember.

"Hey!" A bearded man was kneeling beside me, his arms held out in a mock surrender gesture "Take it easy, pal!" his accent was heavy Bronx, surely a tourist "My name's Jonathan, who are you?"

I stared "Liam."

"You're British?" he sounded surprised.

"English."

"Right. Is this your boat?"

Who else would the half sunk raider belong to? I hadn't the energy to answer his foolish words so I just stared at him.

"When did you last eat?"

That was a good question. I had no idea. I was suddenly aware of a burning, gnawing sensation inside my belly and before I could respond, I doubled over, falling onto my side and retching, dry heaving over the cold stones. A female voice was murmuring soothing words whilst around me other, unseen voices held muted debates over what course of action to take.

"Here..." someone handed me a metal canteen and I drank the waters of the Nahanni greedily, thinking of the gold flakes I'd seen shimmering beneath the icy surface and how the blood of the men on the beach had washed down into the flow...

The water came back up instantly. Now I was heaving in a spasm so strong I felt muscles in my back and core wrenched out of place. Great, seething waves of sickness as though the torturous images that stained my mind could be exorcised with the bile. But the sight of Johannes with his own knife in his eye, Gibbo and his headless torso still chained to the cave, Niimi and the back of his head blown away and then all the others, the dark creature running out of the forest, the awful whistling sounds and underpinning it all, the floating, shimmering flakes of Gold.

"Hey! What's this?"

Inevitable. They'd found the crates Johannes had thrown into the boat. Abruptly, the sickness passed leaving me flat on my back, all my strength burned away. I could hear incredulous voices and rushing footsteps as the tourists opened the crates, discovering the bounty of the Nahanni, the costliest treasure on the earth. I smiled weakly, knowing that this spelled my death. Human charity of course faded in the face of greed and riches. I wondered how many of the group would die before the first canoe breached the end of the river, emerging by the hot springs. Would a bloodied and sickened face, desperately steering a sinking canoe, overburdened by heavy metal stagger into Fort Simpson? Or would the fight take to the river, the rushing waters claiming their bounty once again? I chuckled, the inevitability of it all seeming utterly ridiculous. For some reason, an image of the crisp white linen table cloths decorating the restaurant Adam, Johannes and I had eaten in filled my mind. There had been duck liver pate on the menu I recalled and the man at the table next to me had ordered it. The amount of toast served with the meat had been just right and I'd stared hungrily, wishing I'd ordered the dish.

"You can have it!" I choked out and saw Jonathan staring at me with a wary expression. No wonder. I sounded insane even to my own ears.

"Huh?"

"You can have the gold. I just want some pate."

"Uh… Sure." Jonathan avoided eye contact.

"Hey, Liam?" another voice, this one the female who'd murmured as I was sick. Her face swam into view, young, blonde and a vision of loveliness in this grey, cold pit of despair.

"Hello."

"Hi." she smiled awkwardly "You're a rich man!"

I snorted in derision, turning away. If they were going to kill me then fine. I just wished they wouldn't mock me first.

"Where are the rest of your group?"

What a question that was! I wondered where to start but she moved and behind her, I saw the entrance to a cave, probably the same one that Johannes had climbed inside. I nodded towards it.

"The caves?"

Was that suspicion? Was she trying to determine if the others were coming back? That made me laugh again and my chuckles rang off the rock faces.

"Liam? We need to know if there are any other survivors." it was Jonathan who spoke this time. He and the blonde lady seemed to be taking the lead of their small group.

"You can have the gold!" I insisted, wanting the whole sorry experience to be over.

"What?" she and Jonathan exchanged bemused glances "Liam, no-one is here to rob you! We're gonna help get you out of here! We just need to know where the rest of your group is."

I stared. Was it possible that such charity existed in human hearts? Then again, where had these people come from? Surely, they were just another team that had intercepted Solly's poorly conceived message and come searching the Nahanni for the same false tale as the other teams? But they were civilians, that much was obvious from their garb which was expensive but inefficient. Then there were the straps on their shiny new rucksacks which hung down like the tentacles of a dead octopus. No soldier would allow such a faux-pas.

"Who are you?" I demanded.

Jonathan smiled "I'm Jonathan, this is my wife Chloe and these are our friends. We flew up from Fort Simpson this morning. We're canoeing down the river to the hot springs!"

Although Jonathan looked older than me his words were filled with such joyful exuberance that he seemed to my eyes like a child, boasting of a trip to the seaside or the zoo. Surely this couldn't be a military team in disguise?

"What – what about the fire?" I stammered stupidly.

"The forest fire?" Chloe nodded "Yeah, we came past that. Were those your group's boats?"

I nodded.

"Oh... damn." Jonathan looked pained and I wondered if they'd gone ashore.

"They looked pretty burned up, did the fire catch you by surprise?" Chloe didn't seem to remember that I'd told her my group was in the caves.

"Did you hear the whistles?"

They glanced once at each other, an unreadable look passing between them.

"No. We didn't hear the whistles. What... what do you mean?"

"The creatures..." I tailed off. It sounded ridiculous and there was a growing part of me that didn't believe the entire thing myself "There was something in the caves..."

Chloe and Jonathan turned to look at the cave above us and I saw a flicker of unease pass across them. Jonathan turned away to call to someone else I couldn't see "Hey! How's that repair doing?"

Repair? I couldn't tell what he meant but a moment later a voice called back and Jonathan turned to grin at me.

"Hey, buddy! I think we can get your boat moving again!"

Impossibly, the group managed to make a rudimentary patch on the raider and float it. I was loaded into the hull by many willing hands. There were a dozen or more of the group, American tourists, lovers of the outdoors celebrating Jonathan and Chloe's wedding. Without a flicker of disappointment they strapped their canoes to the side of the raider and loaded me, the Gold and themselves into the boat and set off downstream. Time seemed to blur for me and I stared at the receding walls of the canyons wondering how I was alive.

More to the point, who else was?

Statistically, I should have been dead days ago. Far stronger and more resilient men than me lay headless in second canyon and my broken leg should have spelled my doom but against all the odds, here I was. So, if I was here, someone else must be alive too.

"Did you see anyone?" I murmured and Jonathan, crouching by my side leaned closer to hear me.

"What's that, bud?"

"Did you see anyone at our camp?"

"No." he shook his head "No-one there, dude."

"What about the bodies?"

A stare told me everything I needed to know. I looked to my left, seeing from the low position we sat in the river that the banks which were now opening out wider as we neared the hot springs were mostly hidden. I could see where the water ended but not what lay atop the beaches. I realised that from the canoes, the tourists would have seen nothing but the fire blackened remains of the other two boats.

Jonathan was asking questions but I clamped my mouth shut as a new instinct took over.

Survival.

I realised that I'd been expecting to die for several days now. Gone was the idea of leaving alive and seeing the lights of London or my parents ever again. I'd given myself over to the idea of death, even fantasising about lying as a headless corpse in the valley behind me. But now I was alive and like a burning hot fire being lit in my mind I embraced the idea of survival, life and living. Forget the gold, I was going to make it! Civilisation awaited me, smooth table cloths and all the duck liver pate I could eat! For the first time I looked closely at my rescuers, seeing the innocent care in their faces. I had really and truly come across some genuine hearted human beings who were only out to help a fellow member of the species in my time of need. Tears filled my eyes and Jonathan leaned over me in concern. I grasped his hand.

"Thank you."

He grinned hugely "My pleasure, English!"

The boat was still taking on water and so they ran us aground at the entrance to the hot springs. The familiar stench of sulphur filled my nostrils and for the first time I heard the welcome crackle of a radio as Chloe managed to signal Fort Simpson. She grinned at me, reassuring me that help was on the way.

Not to be distracted, my rescuers stripped into bathing suits and leapt into the warm waters, shouting and shrieking. I stayed on the hard shore, a small smile on my lips as I appreciated for the first time in my life just how wonderful it was to be alive. The happiness and love all around me was the perfect tonic to the days of fear and agony that were now behind me.

Peeeee-hoooo

It didn't scare me. I turned to stare back up the river at the canyons we'd exited but a twist in the river obscured my view. The half smile became a broad grin as the faint whistle died away. It wasn't close and I wondered how many of the creatures had followed our progress down the river and out of their territory. Was that final whistle the all-clear? Or was it a hunting cry, driving the pack out of their lands to bring horror and death to this happy group? As I stared at them frolicking in the sulphur laden water I couldn't believe it. Instead, I turned my body to the direction the faint sound had come from and raised my hand in one final wave of farewell. A salute of parting enemies.

"Hey, Liam! You okay buddy?" Jonathan had been keeping his eye on me, no small feat as his bikini clad wife sprawled next to him, her pale skin glinting in the sunlight. I waved my hand at him, not needing to force the grin onto my face. It was utterly genuine and I nodded to myself as I turned for the last time away from the canyon towards the faint sound of a distant engine as a helicopter clattered towards us to take me home.

CHAPTER 28

London

Perhaps this section of the book should be called a postscript or an epilogue but that doesn't really seem to do justice to the amount I now have to tell and so Chapter 28 it is and shall remain. Firstly, to end the story of the Headless Valley correctly I'll go over a few details to clarify what happened when Jonathan, Chloe and their friends rescued me. A daring helicopter pilot from Fort Simpon agreed to fly me out of there, making a hairy landing on the beach. I went into the cabin with my two crates of gold dust and a grinning Canadian with the most magnificent beard I'd ever seen handed me a bag of food which I began to eat ravenously. As we flew away the Americans waved frantically and as the sunlight reflected on scantily clad bodies, I found myself fervently desiring life above all else.

Back at Fort Simpson I was treated for the myriad injuries. My leg was properly set and a miserable looking old woman who claimed to be a doctor told me the break was one of the cleanest she'd ever seen and that I'd make a full recovery. Then she slapped me with a bill for the treatment which left me wondering if I shouldn't just hand her the gold and be done with it. I had a partially perforated left eardrum, an infected wound on my back that I hadn't even noticed and enough bruising, soft tissue injuries and dehydration that moving was next to impossible for the next week. Fortunately, I was able to contact my parents who reached out to the British embassy and they arrived two days later with a rather fussy middle aged man from the consular staff. He took my statement without comment and then asked a series of rather pointed questions asking me to identify Solly and the rest of my team. I wondered at this, but he wouldn't tell me why and saw no reason not to cooperate.

The real problems, and the reason you're still reading this book, started when a pair of constables from the Royal Canadian Mounted Police came to take my statement. I gave it to them as you've read it here and they made me sign it and date it in front of them before they vanished. That was the last I saw of them and I was able to fly home two weeks to the day after Jonathan and Chloe had rescued me. I was wheelchair bound for another four weeks once the NHS took over my treatment. I wasn't complaining. The restaurant I visited with Adam made space for me and didn't even blink as I ordered six helpings of the pate to my friend's amazement.

I told him the tale and to his credit he didn't interrupt, question me, or even pull a disbelieving face although he looked slightly sickened at the rate I was stuffing pate into my mouth.

"And the Gold?"

Adam turned it into cash for me. Not much, just enough to cover the expenses of the trip and my Canadian hospital bill. I couldn't complain though. I was alive, wasn't I? Adam told me all about the trips where people came back empty handed and so I just shrugged and smiled.

The real kicker came when after I'd been home for about three weeks and was sunning myself in the garden at my parents, my mother opened the back door to usher through a pair of men in the MTP uniforms of British soldiers.

I eyed them warily from my wheelchair seeing at once the distinctive red berets of the Royal Military Police.

"Lance-Sergeant Stryker?"

They introduced themselves as Captain Hacker and Sergeant Poole. I wondered if they were going to finally arrest me for going AWOL before my mobilisation had officially ended and resigned myself to a tedious process of court-martials, stern faced officers and most likely being kicked out the army. Instead, I was dumbfounded when Captain Hacker asked me to provided a statement on the trip to Headless Valley. I already had a copy of the report I'd given to the RCMP and my mother vanished inside the house to find it, handing it over to them. I asked a couple of questions which they didn't answer and they left quickly.

"What was that about?" my mother asked and I shrugged. I'd already spoken to the embassy staff in Canada and they'd assured me that the reports of the SAS men's deaths would be sent to the correct places. As far as I was concerned, my role in the proceedings was over.

But a week or so after the RMP had taken my statement I was visited again. This time I was back at the In and Out club, visiting the on-site physio to begin the laborious process of making my leg muscles function properly again. A pair of smartly suited chaps about my age wearing matching regimental ties that I couldn't place approached me as the physio vanished to wash her hands.

"Liam Stryker?"

"Yes…"

"We were never here. Our job today is to warn you."

I cocked an eyebrow "Warn me?"

"Your expedition to Canada?" it was impossible to tell which of the two men was older. Indeed, they looked so similar they might have been related.

"What about it?"

"You're remaining a free man only on the condition that you never write about, talk about or publish any account of your expedition that includes mention of the following names."

One of the two proceeded to read off a list of names which included the SAS team, the SEALs and finally a handful of hard to pronounce Canadian names which I guessed were the missing natives. Without waiting for an answer, the two men smiled and left leaving me staring after them in shock.

I called Adam. He wasn't a lawyer but he knew what had happened in Canada and I poured out the encounter and to my surprise, he was angry. I'd never marked him as an anti-establishment type but I suppose working in heavily regulated city industries lends itself to a certain type of political persuasion. The long and short of it was that he told me to write this book. Of course there was a huge legal consideration but after the tale of the two spooks threatening me got out, Adam was able to seat me in front of a string of increasingly ardent lawyers who began to string together an argument for my protection. The difficulty was that no-one in an official capacity had approached me and so legally it was all very 'fluid' as one lawyer described it. Still, I sat down and turned this into a book with the help of a few professional writers and within a couple of months we had the story ready to be published.

That's when the Ministry of Defence threw the rule book at me. I was summoned to the HAC where I limped in front of the Commanding Officer to be berated for bringing the army into disrepute. When that elicited little more than an eye roll from me, the Commanding Officer demanded I hand over my ID card and informed me in a formal tone that I would soon be removed from service.

He kicked me out.

Again, this got little more than a shrug from me. I'd had enough adventures for one lifetime and the fact that I hadn't turned up to training in nearly a year was reason enough to oust me from the Reserves. But then began a campaign of discrediting with an efficiency never before seen in the civil service. Firstly, a copy of this book was leaked. The basic story that you've just read made it onto an online message board and spread like wildfire. The internet as usual was torn between scepticism and belief and this only served to fuel the fire of debate. Then the MOD released a denial statement to the clamouring press stating categorically that I'd never been deployed with the SAS, no SAS personnel were considered missing and that I was clearly suffering the effects of PTSD after my mobilisation to Europe.

Notwithstanding the contradiction of admitting I'd been in Europe whilst simultaneously denying I'd mobilised with the SAS, the tide of public opinion soon turned against me. I was now splashed across social media as the uppity STAB, a Walt who lied for attention. Some of it was almost comical in the ludicrous language used but Adam told me to take it all on the chin and get on with finishing the book. Obviously, this is my attempt at getting my own version of events across but doubtless the court of public opinion will try me in the end.

NOTE FROM THE PUBLISHER:

This book is the sole work of Liam Stryker as detailed in the pages here contained. The publisher does not necessarily share the opinions of the author nor are any of the views expressed herein any other than those of the author.

It is our duty at the point of publication to inform the reader that Mr Stryker is currently in detention in Canada where he is charged with the murder of Johannes de Villiers. Whilst Mr Stryker has not been able to release a full statement to describe his experiences thus far, he requested that we, the publisher, explain the abrupt ending to his narrative. Doubtless details of the trial will be shown in the media in the months following publication, but for more information please subscribe to our media channels and our mailing list for updates.

Further, the United States Department of Defense has released a single statement which denies Mr Stryker's claim that members of the US Navy were operating in the region he claims. The loss of US servicemen has not been reported and the veracity of Mr Stryker's claims remains unclear.

Printed in Great Britain
by Amazon

33752296R00112